Fire on the Coastal Road

David Calder

Thank you for reading my work. My books can be obtained either through my website David Calder Books, or from quality brick and mortar and online book retailers.

This is a work of fiction. Names, characters, places, and incidents are either products of my imagination or are used fictitiously. Every effort has been made to respect the privacy of the innocent and unconsultable. Any resemblance to actual persons, living or dead, businesses, companies, events or locales is entirely coincidental.

You can wait for me at the neighborhood coffee shop with latte coffee and a cake on the side
You can wait for me with all the love, but you will wait alone
I am going out just for a moment
Don't say why didn't I warn you earlier
I only went out for a moment
And the tears flow by themselves, to the warm grave.

Yaacov Paz - 'ISRAEL, A NATION OF WARRIORS,' Moshe Katz

Dear Mom and Dad, it is your memorial in a few days, but I don't need that to want to be with you. It's Saturday night and I've just come back from a Shlomi Shabat concert at the Haifa Convention Center. You would have loved the show. I hope you are proud of who I have become. I love you and miss you. Your son who is older than you.

Daniel Bushkenitch, February 2013
Victims of Acts of Terror Memorial in Israel, Mt. Herzl, Jerusalem

Immensely I miss you more each day.

ONE

Cairo, November 11th, 1977
President Anwar Sadat, a nattily dressed, sharp featured man with dark frizzy hair, drew a hush when he rose to speak. He gazed beyond the spotlights, and around the great parliamentary chamber. There was a sprinkling of hijabs and numerous splashes of decorations among at the several hundred delegates and guests. An aide whispered over his shoulder, "The Generals smell something. And the PLO." Sadat nodded.

The date was the 25th anniversary of the 1952 Revolution over the monarchy. Sadat had been a Colonel in the underground Free Officers movement then and played a central part. He spoke effusively about it. Then glossed over financial matters that would have been controversial in greater detail. Finally, he got down to business.

"Members of the People's Assembly, the conflict with our neighbors to the north has produced nothing but bloodshed. If it's not ended, it will mean our irrevocable financial ruin. I will do whatever it takes, even stand up in their Knesset itself to argue with them, if it will prevent one more military casualty or save one more wasted Piastre. Members of the People's Assembly, it is time to make peace with Israel."

The silence was electric. Then applause spread throughout the building, though astonishment abounded. Especially on the grizzled, acne-scarred face of a pudgy 47-year-old, dressed in green fatigues, a black and white checked keffiyeh and scuffed combat boots, named Yasser Arafat. He looked sideways at his chief aide, an Algerian, and whispered in that man's language, "*Mon Dieu, Mon Dieu. Monsieur Sadat qu'avez-nous faith?*" (Mr. Sadat, what have you done?)

The din of hurrying feet broke out as press members scrambling for the public phones.

Jerusalem
In the open-fire-warmed second-floor Prime Minister's Office in the fortified government enclave of Givat Ram, Israeli Defense Minister Ezer Weizman, a brisk-mannered 54-year-old-with a brush mustache and hair receding like Sadat's,

2

raised a hand to quiet the babble of conversation. "It's a ploy. Plain and simple. He can't possibly mean it!"

The four other men present, of similar age except one, said nothing. Each had his own set of opportunities and risks, from Sadat's bombshell announcement, to wrestle with.

"Sadat doesn't really intend to come here," Weizman added. "He's just saying that to look good in Geneva! The Syrians wouldn't consider it for a start. A fragmented Arab bloc plays into our hands, not theirs. Nor will the PLO accept it. They'll fear Jordan and perhaps Lebanon will follow and they'll be excluded."

Yechiel Kadishai, the thin, bespectacled chief of the Prime Minister's Department, said, "I'm not so sure. This endless arms race will bankrupt us all if someone doesn't come to their senses. They can hardly afford to keep up their numbers in Sinai, let alone mount another offensive. We'd be breaking already except for the $3 billion a year from the Americans."

Moshe Dayan, the shaven-headed Minister of Foreign Affairs, smiled. His black eye-patch made it something sardonic. "I don't agree with you at all, Ezer. When you make war on a country twice and get your ass kicked both times, it's not weakness to seek peace. It's common sense. I know. I did most

3

of the kicking. Sadat's a sensible man. I think he's sincere."

"You think?" Weizman replied. "In my experience, when the Arabs say one thing, expect the opposite. Remember their ambush in 1973? I recommend we raise the alert-level at the borders."

Mossad chief Yitzhak 'Chaka' Hofi, standing fireside, grunted. The tall, barrel-chested man was famous for being of few words, and making every one count. "Ezer, you talk as if this was a military problem you can solve with more troops. And by the way, my department knew exactly what was happening before *Yom Kippur.* That's how we wiped out their air forces."

He used his hands for emphasis.

"For me it needs clarifying, I admit we didn't see this coming, but we all saw the signs. As that American song goes, 'you don't need a weatherman to know which way the wind blows.' I say let's wait and see!"

"Well then... Chaka," Weizman sneered, "If I have to do the waiting you better damn well be doing the seeing!"

This tension had always existed between the overt and covert branches of Israel's defense forces.

Hofi lifted a cup of coffee from the mantelpiece and sipped. Slowly, to taunt his rival. "I will certainly do that."

"Ahem," said a gravelly voice. Prime Minister, Menachem Begin, a terrorist in British eyes, and freedom-fighter in others, was in a wheelchair, on medication. He'd developed a heart inflammation while leading his Likud party to power in a huge upset. A fact that kept his many-years-loyal friend Kadishai hovering like a mother hen.

The Prime Minister surveyed the group through round-framed, thick-lensed glasses. "Whether it's a feint, as Ezer says, expedient as Yechiel suggests, common sense as Moshe feels, or something that needs more digging into as Chaka believes, it's an opportunity we must seize! I will receive him."

He paused for breath.

"Yechiel give me a date the Knesset is sitting. Not too soon."

Kadishai consulted a notebook. "The twentieth. Sunday fortnight."

"I will receive him then. If it goes well, I will meet him again with President Carter In the spring. Perhaps March. Let's keep it quiet as long as we can though."

"Yes 'Chem."

"Now, gentlemen, I must rest or endure wrath. Doctors! Pah! What do they know?"

"A lot!" declared Kadishai.

The others bowed their respects and left the room.

Damascus

That evening was cold for November, and the sky gray as steel. Even the famous white minaret above the Umayyad mosque was wreathed in gloom. A fetid smog rose from the central *Souks* (markets) to sting the eyes of the truck drivers on the Ibn al-Abbas highway, before drifting away across the Jebel Aannter hills toward Beirut, 55 miles west.

The view mirrored the moods of the two men watching from a bullet-proof upper window of the PLOs headquarters at Yarmouk Refugee Camp. Both men were stout, with oval northern-Arab features. The shorter of the two, pudgy hands behind his back, uncannily resembled a well-known portrait of Napoleon Bonaparte. In dark suits, white shirts and ties, they might have been bankers instead of mass murderers.

The shorter man, Khalil al-Wazir, had been born in Ramla, Palestine; before the troubles. He preferred his war name, his *kunya*, Abu Jihad, 'Father of the Struggle.' Or his title as Supreme Commander of the PLOs military wing, Fatah.

His companion also went by a kunya, Abu Iyad, meaning 'Power,' but he preferred not to be known at all in public. It wasn't helpful to his role as Fatah's intelligence chief.

Iyad had just explained, "If Sadat makes peace with Israel, best case we'll be marginalized as just

6

another protest group. At worst, our backers will fall like dominoes."

Jihad nodded gravely.

"The big risk is the Americans. Their Jewish-American Democratic voting-bloc wants Middle-East harmony at nearly any cost. They're crucial to Jimmy Carter's re-election in three years' time. He's a much liked, but weak man, and vulnerable on almost all other fronts."

Jihad pursed his lips.

"My contact in the Knesset says Begin wants to meet with Carter in Washington in March. If there's progress between the two countries by then, we can expect an all-out push by the Americans. And the dominoes to tremble."

Jihad said quietly, "We must prevent that if we can, or at least steal the focus if we cannot."

"Yes."

"We will need martyrs," Jihad said.

TWO

Yarmouk

Jihad was back at his office early the following morning. He ordered Iyad, whose office was the foyer to Jihad's suite, to bar all visitors. Then he shut himself away. Just him, and, caffeine addict as he was, his aromatically bubbling Turkish coffee urn.

Soon he was embroiled in thought, but not about Egypt and Israel. He had his own problems. The most pressing involved a woman. And with women and Jihad, sex was most often at the heart of it.

He'd travelled the west extensively since co-founding Fatah 18 years before, promoting the displaced-Arab cause and obtaining weapons. That period included the swinging 60s and half the decadent 70s. His rock star status among the young women of the Middle East wasn't a mystery.

Powerful terrorist leaders lived like the ancient Caliphs, attracting groupies like hummingbirds to nectar. It was a job-benefit Jihad treasured. It didn't worry him for a moment, that the penalty for the women could be death by stoning. He relied on his omnipotence to guarantee conservative women lifted their hijabs above eye-level and kept their gossip within their closest circle, and to ensure that testosterone-engorged fighting men kept their envy to themselves.

Then Dalal Mughrabi entered his life...

He got no further because Iyad entered. Jihad glared.

I should just go sit in the souks and get pestered by the beggars!

"What. Is. It!"

There's more," Iyad said.

"There always is. Can't it wait?"

"Just so long as you know Yasser was there yesterday. In Cairo."

"Well, he'll pester us I'm sure," snarled Jihad.

"Already is. Don't worry. I'll keep him at bay."

"Most apprecia-ted. Now I asked to be alone."

Iyad returned to his desk, where he'd been reviewing reports from his informants. But stung by the humiliation, he set them aside.

Jihad and I have known each other 17, no 18 years. He's a vain, immoral monster. Why do I defer

9

*to him like that? I could run Fatah just as well. And
as ruthlessly.*

But there was something only Iyad could do for
the cause. It was his spies that gave the PLO and
Fatah their edge in the Middle-Eastern politico-
military chess game. That was more important than
ten titles. Without it, the displaced-Arab movement
would shatter into cliques at one another's throats
within weeks. Paralysis would set in. The dream of a
homeland would be over. Iyad shook his head in
exasperation. Jihad and he were inseparable. It was
his calling to serve the cause. And that evil man.

The next report in the stack was from an Amman
merchant. A Jordanian army colonel, a regular visitor
at the merchant's business, had been heard
complaining about his King's constraints against
attacking Israel. The merchant was offering to tape-
record the loose talk for blackmail fodder.

Ever the spider in his lair, Iyad made a note to
follow-up soon.

Jihad poured a fresh cup of coffee the way he liked
it, with a piled spoonful of brown sugar, and went
back to solving his problem.

He'd been absolutely sure no word of their
relationship would reach the powerful and puritanical
leaders he depended on for his status, funding and
Fatah's flow of arms. He'd been spectacularly

wrong. Mughrabi had turned up here in Damascus expecting to be embraced in public. She'd demanded his attention.

Demanded!

He didn't fear losing his trollop-on-the side. Losing the respect of those leaders terrified him. Around them he was... somebody, regardless of what anyone else thought. He'd just completed a successful visit to Moscow. Who'd have imagined that Brezhnev, the all-powerful leader of a 266 million-member empire, kowtowing to a grocer's son expelled penniless from Ramla by the loathsome Jews? No matter that that perverted little lizard, Arafat, had organized it all. It was his militia they feared, not Arafat's.

Jihad thought of his marriage and instantly wished he'd added a pinch of hashish to his coffee. His demure and compliant wife Intissar was also his cousin. That added a whole level of stress if the marriage collapsed. Sharmuta! (bitch)They say Tunisian blood feuds go on forever.

What about his sons, Jihad and Bassem, for whom he had big plans? And his beloved daughters, Iman and Hanan? He'd be ridiculed as a philanderer. Even worse, an incompetent one!

Why? Why me?

He knew THAT answer. His family was a delight to come home to, but his sex drive was enormous. And when it came to fucking, he'd learned

11

enthusiasm was almost everything. Intissar, the perfect Muslim wife, wouldn't understand either word.

He's tried bribery, Allah knew. Mughrabi had rejected a political posting to Rome, outright. Said she wanted to be a fighter like him. And beside him.

Allah please save me.

He had to admit, though, she was remarkable. Nineteen. A trained nurse, and superb with the children at her regular post at Dbaiyeh, north of Beirut. Quite a warrior, having out-trained and out-shot her way to a Lieutenant's commission. Not to mention voluptuous, unlike Intissar's bony build, and exhilarating on a mattress. If she'd only stayed in her place, they might have gone on forever.

Maybe she's a witch. Could I have her shot? No, not so soon after Damascus. It has to be something more subtle.

But he had no more time to spend on this now. There was a war to run, and he had to confront this peace initiative between Egypt and Israel before it smashed down over everything like a breaking tsunami.

THREE

Yarmouk

By the next day, Jihad had a plan formed in his devious mind. It wasn't new thinking.

There was only one thing guaranteed to show Israel how vulnerable it was if it tried to avoid solving the 'Arab Problem.' Terror against its civilians. It didn't need to happen immediately, but he needed such an action in reserve if things moved beyond talk.

Jihad was the master at this. His masterpiece, so far, had been a 1975 assault on the Tel Aviv beach-front that ending with the destruction of the boutique Savoy Hotel, along with eleven Israelis, including an Israeli elite-forces Colonel, no less, and six out of seven attackers.

The challenge was the same every time. Finding people to perpetrate these schemes. You didn't find disciples willing to murder for a cause, and if need be, to die in the process; on just any street corner. And what were you looking for, anyway? The best and brightest? They thought too much. Not that intelligence was incompatible with brutality. Jihad's rivals, the PFLP leaders Haddad and Habash, were medical doctors. What about the worst and dumbest? Would they have the brains and courage to carry it through? Doubtful. Each team had to be meticulously selected, thoroughly trained, and skillfully led.

Jihad's prime advantage was that the Lebanese Civil War, the most fertile terrorism recruiting ground imaginable if the target was the Jewish nation, was being fought just 55 miles away. The war wasn't all Fatah's doing, the region had been a sectarian powder keg for decades. But Fatah fighters had lit the match in April 1975 with an attack on a Catholic church, setting off the years-long cycle of Christian versus Muslim reprisals.

Why was it so ideal?

The war involved thousands of descendants, in their teens through twenties, of the 1948 *Nakba* (Great Catastrophe.) That was the departure or expulsion, depending on which side you were on, of 700,000 Arab occupants of what had been British Mandated Palestine. Those young people were engorged with *Sharifa,* national pride in a nation that had never existed except in the tales told by their refugee parents, loathed Israel fervently, and had no outlet for their grievances.

Better yet, the war was at an uneasy stalemate, with violence only flaring when one militia intruded on the territory of another. That was a marked improvement from the rural atrocities of 1976, such as the butchery at the towns of Aishiyeh and Damour. It gave Jihad complete freedom to recruit. The recruiting places were the displaced-Arab refugee camps, which doubled as Muslim operational bases. The largest, Shatila, occupied most of the Beirut suburb of Sabra. Others were Burj Barajneh, further south near the shell-cratered airport, Dbaiyeh on the northwest coast, and Rashidiyeh, at Tyre in the southwest. Jihad needed volunteers with front-line experience or at least good military training. And that hunger to strike at Israel's heart.

Jihad was limited in his personal movements, overall commander or not. Mossad spies, using aerial and space assets provided by the Americans, hunted him constantly. His motorcade was too juicy a target, and he was too old and proud to hide in car-trunks. He'd have to delegate the initial reaching-out. But he had the perfect man for that. Azmi Zrayir, Commander of the 1500-or-so Fatah *fedayeen* outside of Beirut.

The phone call wouldn't be a pleasure. The man was a sadistic monster, a religious zealot, and an obsequious little fucker who'd lavish him with so many "Allah-bless-you's," he'd have trouble getting a word in edgewise. Jihad wrinkled his nose at the thought. Obsequiousness was often a sign of hidden ambition, and he'd long believed Zrayir would one day become too big for his keffiyeh. But for now, he needed the little bastard.

He picked up the phone and asked the operator at the PLO security center to find Zrayir and get him on the line.

Tyre, Lebanon

At that moment, in a town on the Mediterranean coast, the morning sky was leaden, and an icy wind mischievous, among a battalion of men arrayed in stiff ranks across the main square. On a dais in front was a uniformed man with his hands bound, blinking blood from his eyes after a gun-butt interrogation, and sweating heavily.

Captain Fouad Mansour knew he was a dead man. He'd seen too many of these charades, never imagining he'd one day be the guest of honor. Behind him stood a masked fighter in fatigues, holding a Kalashnikov against Mansour's battered ribs.

His inquisitor beside him was a short, fiery eyed, hawk-nosed man, wearing a snowy traditional-

Bedouin robe topped by Fatah's black-and-white checked keffiyeh.

"You are a filthy Israeli spy!" shrieked Azmi Zrayir. He held up the evidence of Mansour's treachery on high. A miniature copy of the Druze bible found during a surprise barracks inspection. Sunni Arabs, which meant most of Fatah's forces, hated the Druze for their friendly relations with the Jews.

"All Fatamids are filthy spies," said Zrayir, now face to face with his quivering victim. "Admit it or I will have your tongue cut out!"

Mansour's lips went paper-dry. That was so idle threat. "I... no, my Colonel. Yes, I am of the *al-Muwahhidin*, but I have served Fatah well. These men will tell you that!"

Zrayir turned to 'those men.' They stood rigid; eyes fixed straight ahead. He smiled, relishing his role as Allah's avenger. "Is that so? Who speaks for this Fatimid? Come forward and join him!" There was only a swirl of dust on the malevolent breeze.

That was enough of a lesson for one day, Zrayir decided. He was bored. If he had the time, he'd chain his victim's feet to the bumper of a Technical, a Toyota Hilux pickup with a machine gun bolted to the bed, and have the driver circle the square. Much more satisfying.

He gestured with one hand. The rifle touched the back of Mansour's head, but he never heard the

17

explosion. His brains splashed out across the cobblestones.

After a lingering silence, during which Zrayir scanned the rows of faces for dissent, the troops dispersed. Zrayir was immediately summoned to the phone in a small office off the square.

Jihad said what he needed, ending with, "I'll be relying on you for logistical support too, Azmi. Security, launching facilities, weapons and equipment."

"Allah bless you for giving me this trust, Effendi."

"I have told you before Azmi, I'm not your Lord. We are all equals under the banner of Fatah."

"Forgive me, Eff... I will not let you down!"

I guarantee you that!

"Why at my headquarters, I have such a man now," Zrayir offered. "A fisherman's son from Batroun, Mahmoud Ali Naif. Only 22, but capable and a good leader. He's recovering from minor wounds."

Well, he at least knows men.

"I will give it thought, Azmi, and perhaps meet with this man. Keep him around your camp for now."

"As you wish Effendi."

Jihad grimaced in irritation, but let it pass.

"And I do. In the meantime, have details of all suitable candidates sent to Damascus."

"Allah bless you, Effendi."

"And you Azmi."

FOUR

Yarmouk

Jihad was kept occupied the following week, dealing with a thwarted Muslim drive east from the Green-line that divided Beirut. On the Friday, though, at the regular end-of-week round table, he asked Iyad what his spies were hearing about Egypt and Israel. Iyad obfuscated.

"You'll recall we fired Katyusha rockets over the Lebanon border into Nahariya last week. Word is there were more casualties than the Israelis admitted."

"Excellent," said Jihad to nods all around the table. "If we have the ammunition, we should keep that up."

"Might want to be careful, though," Iyad added, "Weizman threatened in the Knesset on Monday to carpet-bomb our launch area if we do it again."

"Let's give it some time then. What about the TV appearance you were talking about?"

"Yes. Walter Cronkite had Begun and Sadat on his CBS News Hour by satellite. They talked about negotiations with 'no prior conditions.' You know what that's shorthand for!"

"Yes. Throwing us on the scrap-heap."

Iyad hesitated. His boss was going to get angry.

"Begin has sent a formal invitation to Egypt for a Sadat state visit. Egypt has accepted."

"Ebn El Sharmuta!" (SOB) Jihad roared. "I was hoping it was all just talk. What's the date?"

"The 19th of February. On their *Shabbat*"

"Khara!"

"Sorry. Only learned about it this morning. We could organize a reception..."

Jihad seethed for a moment. "No. Not enough time. What else?"

"The Israelis that matter have mixed views. Army Chief of Staff Mordechai Gur has accused Egypt of a secret buildup of forces. On the other side, Dayan was on the radio on saying Israel should welcome the Egyptian change of position after 29 years. Overall, there's relief. Not good."

What's that American saying? La khara Sherlock?

"Well, keep me advised."

Iyad said, "I'll do that."

The following day a worn looking Begin addressed his formerly bitter enemies on black-and-white television. Jihad watched from his fortified villa at Yarmouk.

"Citizens of Egypt. This may be the first time I speak to directly, but not for the first time I think of you. You are our neighbors and always will be. We the Israelis, stretch out our hand to you. It is not a weak hand. If attacked we shall always defend ourselves. Your president has said he is ready to come to Jerusalem. It will be a pleasure to welcome him with the hospitality you and we have inherited from our common father, Abraham. If we all act in good faith, I will be glad to come to your capital Cairo for the same purpose. No more wars. Peace. A real peace and forever."

Jihad's troubles were deepening, for certain. But then, so was his resolve. And there should still be plenty of time.

On Saturday evening the 19th of February 1977, as the third and Shabbat-ending star blinked to life over the Sinai Desert, many watching saw something they'd believed impossible.

An Egyptair passenger jet entered Israeli airspace unmolested. The six MIGs escorting it peeled away to the south. The same number of Kfir fighter jets joined it for the rest of its journey. Sadat descended the aircraft's stairs at Tel Aviv's Ben Gurion airport. Begin embraced him. Crowds cheered. Brass bands blared. A 21-gun salute thundered.

The next morning in the Knesset in Jerusalem, Begin feted Sadat as a long-lost friend. "We welcome you and honor your courage. Everything can be negotiated, and must be negotiated."

Iyad's bulletins over the next while described a river of congratulatory and conciliatory messages between the two nations. Opposition Leader Peres supported the government. President Katzir joined in. Golda Meir praised the initiative despite having once said, "We will have peace when they love their children more than they hate us."

Dayan proposed Egypt-Israeli talks in Geneva to build on the disengagement agreement signed after the 1973 Yom Kippur War. Sadat offered discussions in Cairo. President Jimmy Carter sent Secretary of State Cyrus Vance for support in the second week of December. Begin made a surprise visit to Washington to plead Israel's case.

It was a nightmare-come-to-life for Jihad. Despite his vicious soul and complete control of the foreign-aid millions Fatah received, he'd never enriched himself. That was looking like very bad management. He could see the comfortable retirement he'd always imagined, basking in the glow of securing a homeland for his people, shrinking to a miserable existence in a 100-peso-a-month Cuban tenement, watching over his shoulder for the icepicks like Leon Trotsky.

He doubled-down on his planning.

A month later, Iyad entered Jihad's office to see his boss reviewing dossiers at the conference table. Each had a large photo of a man in battle-gear pinned to the cover. Jihad growled, "Tell me the good news."

"There isn't any unless you are counting on the UN to be practical, in which case you most probably believe in djinns."

"Oh? What's their latest fantastic plan?"

"The usual number-soup. Resolutions 32/20 and 32/40. Full recognition of Palestinian rights."

"And they plan to invade Israel to impose those, of course?"

"The resolutions will die in the Security Council from a U.S. veto, as always."

"What a surprise!" Jihad said. He pointed at the sprawl of documents. "Anyway, I wanted your view on these."

Iyad stepped to the table. "That's your shortlist? Zrayir looks like he's done well."

"I'm calling it Operation Kamal Adwan."

That didn't need clarifying. Adwan, the PLO spokesman killed in a 1973 Israeli commando raid, had been a friend of both men.

Iyad pretended to study the cover photos and names. He knew every detail. Everything crossed his desk whether Jihad knew it or not. "I don't see the big Syrian, Ahmadi."

"Killed at Jounieh last week."

"Pity. What about the South American, Rodriguez?"

"He's crazy. Threw a grenade at a couple of comrades at a roadblock. I'm having him shot."

Iyad took a seat. "The rest all seem okay. Except one. I know several of them, like that big Kuwaiti camp guard at Shatila."

The spymaster picked up a file bearing the picture of a slim, arctic-eyed youth. That youth had executed a traitor unmasked at a PLA-Fatah meeting, right there at the table. "I was at that meeting. An emotional boy, but he does cold-blooded work!"

"Pleased to hear," Jihad said. "The Gazans and the West Bankers look capable. I'm not sure about the boy from Ramallah, from those riots, but I'll interview him. Which one worries you?"

Iyad's jaw set rock hard. "You know very well which one, Khalil. He's been nothing but trouble. It's all I can do to stop scar-faced Mohammed from cutting his throat in an alley!"

"His parents were like family," Jihad said. "I put him into intelligence because I thought he had promise. He did well in Tel Aviv, didn't he?"

"Yes, he did," admitted Iyad.

"Well this will solve your problem then, won't it?"

Iyad agreed with that too.

FIVE

Beirut

Monday morning dawned drizzly and gray in the city once called the 'Paris of the Middle East' but which was now just the shelled-out detritus of a bitter war.

Jihad had traveled overnight along a circuitous route from Damascus to Shatila Camp. As the city came to life, he had himself chauffeured to a row-house on a street less graffiti-plastered than most of the Sabra District.

Wearing the dark double-breasted suit that was as much his trademark as Arafat's fatigues, boots, and keffiyeh, and with his driver holding an umbrella above his head, he climbed spider-cracked steps in front and knocked. It felt quaint. It was at least 20 years since he'd asked permission. For anything.

A middle-aged woman named Louha Mughrabi answered. She lifted her black shawl over hers head and bowed. Several dark-haired children playing in the lounge ran away giggling. Mrs. Mughrabi called out deeper into the house and stepped aside. A hallway doorway opened a few inches and a young woman's face peered out. Jihad marched to the door and closed it behind him. Dalal Mughrabi stood illuminated by a pale light leaking in through closed lace curtains. Jihad sat on the foot of the rumpled bed.

Dalal was undoubtedly attractive, with her face framed by wavy dark hair cut pageboy style. Her intense, almost obsidian eyes were windows into a spirit Jihad knew had uncommon determination. Her shapeless nightgown couldn't conceal her fitness and strength. He remembered the small breasts with pert upstanding nipples, the curves of her thighs and the soft woman parts between them. And her writhing beneath him. Her cries of lust in the night. Part of him wondered how he might maneuver her onto her knees before him, even now.

She stared back defiantly.

Jihad said, "How are you little one?"

"I am well *Umri*." She always used the endearment, 'my life,' when they were alone. "But I miss you."

"I understand," he said. "But circumstances..."

"I want to be with you," she blurted.

"Alas, you cannot."

"You would rather be with that... woman?"

27

"Intissar and my children are not something we can speak of, little one. They are part of me and cannot be separated."

She flared. "Am I not part of you too Umri?"

He raised a hand. "We have had much, little one. But it must end now as I told you in Damascus when you came unannounced."

"I needed you! I had to see you!"

Jihad sighed. "Little one, I deal with powerful men. Conservative men. They wouldn't understand."

Dalal sobbed.

"I am a leader. I must suppress my own needs." He extended an olive twig, "Though it breaks my heart to do so."

He stood and said more firmly, "And I must think of my children. My son Jihad will replace me someday, Allah willing."

Dalal saw she'd lost the argument. "I only want to serve the cause and fight the Jews beside you, and in your..."

"That has ended!" Then Jihad softened. "But if you wish to fight the Israeli dogs, you can do so with your training and leadership. I plan an operation."

She brightened. "I will serve you any way I can."

"Then that is the way. I will send for you when I return to Damascus. But what we had must be behind us now. Do you accept that?"

She studied the floor. "Yes."

"Again, so I am sure."

"Yes."

"Good. I will send for you. Be ready." He marched out.

Dalal slumped on the bed, weeping wretchedly.

Jihad's concerns about Mughrabi ruining his life, now at bay, he started interviewing the men Zrayir had put forward for Operation Kamal Adwan.

The first was the baby-faced but hard-eyed, 18-year-old Jordanian named Mustapha Abu Ramez, whom Iyad had remembered.

"*Alhamdulillah* (praise be to God), during the Nakba my father Ibrahim fought for Fawzi al-Qawuqji, a great soldier," He said.

Jihad marked him as religious, a problem if overdone.

Ramez told of his father coming home during a break in the assault on the kibbutz of Mishmar HaEmek. The house had been dynamited and the man's first wife and baby daughter were dead in the rubble.

"*Inna lillahi wa inna ilayhi raaji'oon* (surely we belong to Allah and to him we will return)," Jihad sympathized.

Ramez told other stories of Israeli brutality and injustice. Jihad had heard them all. They became repetitive after a while. He reviewed Ramez' military record while paying half-attention. The youth had

29

been a bodyguard to several senior PLO figures and was a natural with any weapon. The file warned about a viperlike temper, but said he was a fervent Jew-hater and utterly remorseless. He suited Jihad's needs well.

Jihad asked young Ramez to choose a kunya. Ramez chose Abu 'Rami,' the 'Gunman.' Jihad thought that was an enlightened choice.

Dbaiyeh, on the north Mediterranean, was a camp Jihad liked. He'd met Dalal Mughrabi there. This time he met a hulking, brutish, 21-year-old Gazan named Zukhair al-Massri. An actual 'Palestinian,' born the only year Gaza wasn't owned by one power or another.

Al-Massri described pitched battles of his childhood in Khan Yunis' Palestine Square. Rocks against IDF rubber bullets. He'd been smuggled out by Bedouins through a tunnel into the Sinai before he was old enough to be imprisoned or executed. He'd found his way to Lebanon via Cairo and Cyprus, and joined the *Ain Jalut*, a Syrian-aligned militia accused of numerous atrocities.

"Yes, I've been to the villages and killed the *Masiheyin* (Christians.) Now I'm with Fatah."

"Why are you here today?

Al-Massri showed a mouthful of gapped-teeth and made an over-arm motion. "I'd like to throw stones at the Jews again. I'm much better at it now."

He ironically chose Abu 'Jalal,' meaning 'Seeker of Glory,' as his war-name.

There was a dozen more at different locations, bearded and straggly haired to a man, often in miss-matched battledress, but all wearing black-and-white Keffiyehs. Some were rejected out of hand, as posers and wannabees.

Among the selected was 19-year-old Amer Ahmed Amreya, an exiled student-activist from the West Bank. He prattled on about political ideology and revolutionary idols, some of whom Jihad counted as friends, though he didn't say so for fear of extending the conversation. With a rare lack of humility, Amreya took on the name of 'Tariq,' the 8th-century Muslim conqueror of Spain.

Another was a stammering 18-year-old Jordanian named Mohammed Hussain al-Shamri, from a wealthy home but a veteran ragamuffin and thief from among the souks of Amman. It seemed he was good at it, because he still had both his hands. He became 'Hussain' for the mission.

Eighteen-year-old Khaled Hussein, an oil-worker's son from Kuwait, was gangly and raw like an overgrown boy, with thick lips and scruffy facial hair. He's been called up from the among the buildings, and sniper nests, of the Beirut Green Line. He struck Jihad as a little dim-witted, but his record was steady and should make a good follower. Hussein wishfully chose his first name Abu 'Khaled' meaning 'Immortal.'

Jihad met that the last candidate available for the time being, on the 23rd December at Shatila.

Fawzi al-Ramez, from Jericho, carried his 225 pounds with brooding menace. He had a bandaged upper-arm wound and was missing his front teeth. At 24 he was the oldest prospect and the most experienced fighter. As with Jalal, he'd started out as a stone thrower during street uprisings against Israeli occupation.

He must have been what? Thirteen when the Jews seized the West Bank in the 1967 war? Who from that time WASN'T heaving rocks?

But unlike Jalal, he'd been too stubborn or inept to escape before reaching imprisonment age, and had done serious Israeli prison time. His eyes glittered as he described his capture and a rock the size of his fist. "I got one as they came at me though. Between the eyes."

"Where did they take you?"

"To Camp Ofer, for indefinite detention."

Jihad pictured the barbed wire, rough prefabricated buildings, and harsh climate of the notorious camp at Giv'at Ze'ev near *Al-Quds* (Jerusalem). "That's a tough place at seventeen."

The big man shrugged. "The Jews called us *Metmurds.* (Intransigents.) We were caged 24-hrs a day. They enjoy the *Falaka* at Ofer too."

Beating of the soles of the feet until raw. Jihad shuddered.

"I used to dream of getting my hands around one of their throats, just once," Al-Ramez mused. "But they never come close enough of course."

"Never?"

"We used to save our khara." The big ugly man made a throwing motion.

The final defense of the utterly defenseless. Throwing your own shit at your enemy. "Not even to feed you?"

Al-Ramez' eyes darkened to the color of his soul. "Three Jews came twice a day. Two with riot shields. One with buckets of wheat slush. They'd pour the buckets into a channel like for rainwater on a house. Lift one end with a stick so it ran down to us. The way you'd feed pigs. Thirty of us in a cage. Ten cages. We'd scoop it up with our fingers. The weak did not eat often."

"Water?"

"They'd turn on a hose twice a day too."

Allah's mother.

"And they released you in the prisoner exchange in 1976?"

33

"Yes. I crossed the *Urdunn* (Jordan) and volunteered at Karameh."

He mentioned a well-known Fatah officer at that Jordanian base famous for the armored confrontation that put the PLO on the political map in 1968.

"He sent me to Beirut to kill the *Masiheyin*. (Christians) They say I do it well. I've certainly done it enough. Believe me, they are no substitute for Jews."

"What war-name would you like to use?"

"Ramz. Just Ramz."

Symbol of freedom. "Very well."

"*Insha'Allah* (as Allah wills.)" When do we begin?"

"Soon. Very Soon."

SIX

Yarmouk

Back in Damascus, Iyad had also just returned from a covert mission. Visiting his spies in Lebanese Prime Minister Karami's government. Jihad demanded the latest news.

"We are having a few wins at the U.N."

"Not that it matters," Jihad said, irritated as always by the mention of the feckless world body. "The Americans quash them all."

"Not all. The resolution against terrorism came to a vote."

"The security council's been pushing that a long time. It's not in our interests either."

"True, but our Russian friends put in a clause excluding any 'national liberation movement.' We're esteemed freedom fighters now."

Jihad snorted. "Yasser will be ecstatic. How are things between Egypt and the Jews?"

"More talks start Saturday. At Ismailia in the Canal Zone this time. Hopefully just another talk-fest that won't produce a thing."

"I'm not so sure," Jihad said morosely. "The more they talk, the more chance they'll agree on something. Begin's getting too proactive for my liking. We need him back home, focused on his own backyard."

"We'd better speed up this action of yours then."

Jihad scowled. "I'm working on it."

A political crisis flared up before Jihad made any more headway. An army-patrolled buffer zone had been proposed in refugee-swollen south Lebanon. The last thing Jihad wanted near the Israel border. He had to call in most of his markers with his contacts in the Syrian Government to get it canceled No sooner was that cleared up, when Iyad came into his office very concerned.

"Begin has pulled... what's that basketball term, a full court pressure. He's at Ismailia with Dayan, Weizman, and his Attorney General, making proposals."

"And?"

"It's succeeded. Joint military and political committees start meeting mid-January."

Jihad's mind raced. He'd expected more time. Zrayir would have to vet and approve the candidates outside Yarmouk. Those were a Yemini at Dbaiyeh, one Egyptian at Karameh and another in Nahr al-Bared on the Lebanese coast. Or not. He sent orders to Tyre.

That left a man Jihad knew him far too well. The same man Iyad objected to.

Abdul Salaam was a 19-year-old fisherman's son from Tripoli. Slim, charming and handsome, with a Charlie Chan mustache and a pretentious Afro. He might cut a dashing figure under the silver balls of Damascus' discotheques, but he was also an arrogant, womanizing pain in the ass. When Abdul was at the University of Tripoli, two years past, his father was shot by a nervous IDF conscript while entering the West Bank on a family visit. He'd quit school and begged his 'Uncle' Khalil for a job. He'd been studying languages, so was given two weeks of Hebrew training, then smuggled into Tel Aviv on reconnaissance. He was now doing propaganda and money-collection in the building right next door to Jihad's HQ, where he had alienated everyone in his section in record time. Then capped that off with an affair with the wife of a mid-level Fatah commander. The wastrel had volunteered for Kamal Adwan because the alternative was winding up dead in the street.

But he was the only man on Jihad's list who was both Hebrew-speaking and had actually seen Israel. If he could be fitted in, his contribution could be vital.

Also, the operators would be entering Israel by sea. As a fisherman's son, Abdul must have some boating experience.

He sent word that Abdul was to stand by and noted on his plan to call him Abu 'Salaam.' Then he turned his focus to leadership.

Jihad's HQ was under assault by wicked weather two days later, with sleet rattling at window panes, and crusty ice on the sidewalk. Lieutenants Mahmoud Ali Naif and Dalal Mughrabi got down from a brown Unimog truck in their olive-green battle fatigues, combat boots, and keffiyehs They knew very well that this summons likely meant their deaths.

After stamping some circulation back into their feet, they surrendered their Kalashnikovs and Makarovs at the guard station. Clumped up the staircase to the second floor.

Jihad kept the pair waiting while he pulled together his thoughts. His mind was on a previous time with important similarities.

In 1970, PFLP combat teams, led by a young woman named Leila Khaled, shocked the western media with a series of airplane hijackings. They'd flown three airliners to Dawson's Field in the Jordanian desert and blown them up. That had set off the Jordanian Black September War, a disaster for the PLO, but Leila Khaled's charisma and contempt for western authorities had shown the world what a dedicated woman could achieve for a cause.

Jihad needed that kind of dedication if he was to derail the Egypt-Israel peace initiative before the Americans got so involved there'd be no stopping it. Mughrabi was here partly because she was the perfect stand-in for Leila Khaled. But that shrank to insignificance at the thought of her being out of his life forever. She was impossibly tenacious. She'd never let him have a life without her. Not this life of unadulterated power.

He waved them in and summoned Iyad. The temperature was freezing inside as well. The terrorist leaders wore greatcoats over their suits. Mughrabi adopted the 'at-attention' military stance she knew was expected, and after a moment's hesitation Naif followed suit.

Jihad, hands clasped behind his back, circled them slowly; something he did habitually to disconcert. Dalal looked to have put their past behind her, holding herself erect and looking straight ahead. Naif seemed to be smirking. Smirking. Only a fool with a death wish did that here.

Naif had impressed Zrayir. Jihad could see how the man might make a good first impression. He was tall and strong, also fair-haired and blue-eyed, unusual for an Arab. And he must have performed well enough to have earned a commission. But his references told a different tale. His couldn't-care-less attitude, constant joking around, and pitiful need to be everyone's friend, grated on those around him. And he sulked when caught in one of his frequent lies.

Still, he was there and Jihad was out of time. And he had sea-faring experience. He might shape up during advanced training. Jihad put his misgivings aside.

"I have brought you here to offer you a great opportunity to serve the cause." Jihad knew he was straining his credibility. Fatah never 'offered' anyone anything.

"I understand you know boats." he asked Naif.

Naif grinned. "Hard not to if you want to fish for bream in 60 feet of water."

Jihad stopped still. The man had no situational sense. A long silence hang in the room while he considered having Naif taken down in the basement and shot.

To his credit, Naif blurted, "Yes Sire! My father was a fisher. I crewed with him many times. I often ran the boat while he prepared the catch."

"Good. Good, because we plan to strike a blow at the Jews' own hearts, from the sea. But Mahmoud." Jihad clapped his hand on Naif's shoulder. "Do not call me Sire. We are all brothers in the cause here."

"We have selected a force," he went on. "Two teams, and we plan to deliver them by ship under your joint command, to just off *Yáfa.* (Tel Aviv.) From there you will sail to shore in smaller craft and seize a large hotel and hostages. You will trade those first for foreign ambassadors, and then for our brothers in Jewish jails and your freedom to return home to the honors that will be due to you."

He moved in front of Dalal

"Sister I need much from you. You will be my Warrior Queen and strike a blow for your sisters. They need to see that it's not just our men who bear our flag, but all of us. Will you do that?"

Dalal was under Jihad's spell once again. He'd re-awoken the dreams of her childhood. She had imagined this moment every day since she'd joined Fatah.

Naif had drawn himself up an inch or two, swelled with pride. Here was his chance at heroism. "We will not fail you."

"Good. Good, come let me show you." They moved over to the maps. One was of the Tel Aviv waterfront.

"I don't know this place," Naif said.

"One of your team has been there, and will show the way."

Jihad pointed out the places they needed to know about.

41

"The Zionist pig Begin plans meetings in America with the dog Carter within the next few months. No later than *Bahá* (late March.) We must show them they cannot just speak with whom they wish about betraying us. And that they'll never be safe in their beds until they meet our demands for nationhood."

He grasped Naif's shoulder. "I am honored to serve with you, Mahmoud. You will be our commander while at sea, and lead our brave warriors to the Zionists' shore, where," He punched his right fist into his left palm, "We will strike!"

Words are cheap. Actions will decide in due course.

"Sister Dalal you will be our flag-bearer when on land. You will carry it high into the dens of our enemies!"

She beamed. Naif looked ready to explode with pride.

"Comrades, I know you will not fail me or the martyrs before you. But this must be kept entirely secret. This action will be called 'Kamal Adwan' after our comrade martyred in Beirut. Your training will begin within days. Your men are on their way to join you. There is no god but Allah, and Muhammad is his messenger."

The two filed out, eyes gleaming. The weather had worsened. A truck-journey might be fatal. They left Yarmouk in a Chevy Caprice.

Within minutes, Jihad had sent a messenger after them to request aliases. Naif's choice of Abu 'Hiza'a,' showed imagination. Khirbet Hiza'a is the name of a fictional Arab village from the time of the Nakba, in an expose-book written by a non-conformist Jewish writer named S. Yizhar. Naif might be a lightweight, but he wasn't illiterate.

Dalal Mughrabi chose, simply, 'Sister Dalal.'

Jihad stayed up late sending out special orders before retiring to his suite on Loubia Avenue to let things unfold.

SEVEN

Yarmouk

Within a further few days, Jihad had his information on the remaining three candidates.

The 18-year-old Yemeni, Akram al-Assadi, was of the Al-Matheel people from the mountains south of Sana'a. He had the wiry build, beak nose, wispy beard, and dark curly hair growing out of control, of most men from those wild tribes. Also, the friction mark called a *Zebiba*, from frequent contact between his forehead and a prayer mat. Those could be the signs of a dangerous fanatic. So was the traditional *Jamiyah* (dagger) he'd worn to his interview. But knowing the Yemeni fighting reputation, Zrayir had approved him, Jihad was glad to have him. He noted al-Assadi had adopted one of the 99 names of the Prophet Mohammed, Abu 'Ahmed,' as his war-alias.

The Egyptian at Karameh, Mohammed Raji al-Sheraan, another 18-year-old with a deluge of dark hair, bulbous nose, and thick lips, had also impressed Zrayir with his willingness and enthusiasm, despite his inexperience. He requested Abu 'Wael,' the 'Rescuer,' as his kunya.

It was the other Cairo-raised man the same age, Hussein Fayadh, who was a problem. He hadn't been interviewed at all. Zrayir hadn't had time to get to Nahr al-Bared. Jihad had to go off the man's file. It described a small, insecure, dislikeable but slyly clever boy, with a perpetually shifty expression. At his interview on joining the cause, Fayadh had claimed to be inspired by the writings of martyred Jihadist, philosopher and founder of the Muslim Brotherhood, Sayyid Qutb. He gave 'family reasons,' common code for an upbringing filled with horror stories of the Nakba, for traveling to Beirut. The fact he was serving in Nahr al-Bared, a shit-hole as far from the action as one could get, might have given him away as a coward. Jihad would have rejected him if he'd met him, but he needed one more soldier and accepted him. He became plain 'Fayadh.'

On the last day of 1977, Jihad and Iyad met to talk about where the commando force should train. Iyad agreed enthusiastically with Jihad's first suggestion .

"Damour? I know it well. Good choice!"

All the Middle East and most of the west had heard of Damour. The previous year, PLO-aligned forces had swooped from the eastern hills and assaulted the Christian township 15 miles south of Beirut. The attackers, including Syrians from the As-Sa'iqa (Thunderbolt Brigade) under Zukhair Mohsen, who would ever after be known as the 'Butcher of Damour,' overwhelmed the town garrison. They rounded up the Christian townsfolk, 582 men, women, and children, and machine-gunned them against alley-walls.

Iyad elaborated on his enthusiasm. "The Masiheyin had a barracks and training area in the valley between the highway and the hills. With the refugees we've moved into the town, we can pass our men off as guards, or even social workers. A perfect location I would say."

"I will tell Zrayir to make it happen," said a pleased Jihad. "And what about other matters?"

"Things seem quiet Khalil. Just the usual political posturing going on."

Iyad was lying. A dangerous practice around Abu Jihad, but he had good reason.

Sadat's peace tender had enraged the Soviets. It threatened their Middle East influence. The KGB had met in Baghdad with Abu Nidal, an independent terrorist leader known to be a crazy drunk, and Ilich Ramirez Sanchez, the famous Carlos. They offered a huge sum for a credible attempt on Sadat's life. Carlos had dismissed it as a suicide mission, but

Nidal had taken the money. Nidal's group might not get the job done, but he was insane enough to try.

The intelligence chief wasn't keeping this to himself because the information was in doubt.

It would bring out the worst in his boss. Iyad managed this aspect of the Fatah leader with great care. If he told Jihad, his boss would first rub Iyad's nose in Nidal's willingness to do something he wouldn't. Iyad didn't enjoy being humiliated. Then he'd drive all those around him to distraction with his schemes and counter-schemes. Better to keep his mercurial boss's focus on this Israeli venture, which actually looked like it might bear fruit.

Also, Nidal and Iyad had been blood enemies since a split between Fatah and Nidal's forces. Nidal had made at least three attempts that kill him. What if Nidal actually got to Sadat? That suited Fatah so long as their fingerprints weren't on it. And if world opinion shifted, and it looked to be unwise? Iyad was sure he could derail it fairly easily. *Come to think of it, I might even disrupt the damn thing just to spite the man.*

Jihad rose in dismissal, "Well, please keep me informed of anything you hear."

"You can bet on that," Iyad said.

Jihad cut several sets of fresh orders. One was to Zrayir to have the Damour training site repaired, provisioned, and otherwise made ready for immediate use. Another was to go out simultaneously to an apartment within Yarmouk Camp and a barracks in Beirut.

This left only the selection of the force's trainer to make Operation Kamal Adwan irrevocable. The man he had in mind was right-then supervising a crucial arms delivery into the Beirut docks. Mohammed Mahmoud Abdul al-Raheem Masameh.

At 29, Masameh was an old man in militia circles. Old enough to be a 'true' Palestinian, born in Yáfa before the Nakba. Over six feet in height and sculptured, his good looks, topped by a mane of dark hair, were blemished only by two missing fingers from his left hand. It was a badge of honor earned in the 'Black September' fighting in Jordan in 1971.

He was a veteran of Fatah's elite *Al-Asifah* squad (The Young Lions,) and past commander of Yasser Arafat's Force 17 personal guard. After that, he was too valuable to risk on just any battlefield. Jihad had made him roving inspector of the camps, finding promising fighters he could up-skill, and weeding out recruits with no chance of making the grade. Losing him for the time required for training would be difficult, but he was hands-down the best man for the task.

Jihad leaned back in his chair and considered what he'd accomplished.

His fighting force was twelve strong, some experienced at war, others with definite fighting potential. There were zealots, but also moderates, and some with no religion at all except the sermon of the gun. All bound by the blood in their veins and the hatred for Israel in their hearts.

All they need is Masameh's firm guidance, and may Allah help anyone who defies them.

He wrote one more order, collected the others together, and summoned an aide. "Deliver these overnight. Tell those receiving them to act immediately."

Operation Kamal Adwan was under way.

EIGHT

Middle East

Nineteen seventy-eight dawned icy-bright but quiet across the Levant. Devout Muslims, or those wise to appear so, don't celebrate New Year's Day. Sunday was just another working day.

Salaam was in bed in his second-floor apartment on Yarmouk's Palestine Avenue. He was thinking about dumping a young girl whose name he didn't care to remember and walking to his office for an early start. Then there were boots on his stairs. Hiza'a got his orders the same way at Shatila. The two were soon on their separate ways to Latakia, on the Mediterranean, 200-odd miles north of Damascus.

They got there in the evening, to an amphibious-training school on the Al-Orouba docks. Their arrival at a dormitory triggered a barrage of curses, like a shouting match at the tower of Babel;

"What the fook! što je jebote? Yeah mate what the fucking hell," before all settled down again.

The following morning a fat, balding, Syrian naval-officer named Galal Abdalla Ali, told them to not to ask questions, but mind their own business, which would take two weeks. He sent them to a noisy warehouse reeking of exhaust fumes, where outboard motors puttered away in water tanks along one wall. Five men from the dormitory were under instruction. One instructor gave directions in Arabic. Another in thick eastern-European accented English.

When their turn came, they learned to strip, reassemble and restart, even in the dark, the primitive but functional Russian Mockba-M16HP military-issue two-stroke motor. For added spice, there were sometimes flash-bangs exploding in the background, excessive oil in the gasoline, or a bucket of salt water had been poured through the workings.

Once they'd mastered those challenges, they spend days at the beach alongside the wharves, training in groups of six, on the Czech made, Zverokruh (Zodiac) inflatable boat. Each drab-gray craft was 14 feet by six-and-a half-wide. Lettering on a patch next to the engine mount said it could carry up to seven men and 1650lbs total weight if properly balanced.

Their teammates were a pair of Turks from the Party of Liberation, an Italian from the Red Brigades, and a Kosovan from some unpronounceable Muslim separatist group. They had to communicate in whispers because anything louder drove the supervising Syrians into a rage.

Among the tricks learned was carrying the empty boat by ropes along the sides, a hundred yards at a run without stopping. And launch-and-recovery, via davits attached to the dock to simulate a mother-ship. Before operating the boat by engine, they had to prove they could handle it using the three pairs of collapsible oars. The week was stormy in the northern Mediterranean and there were many capsizes. The boat was stable and nimble under power during the final sea exercises. The Soviet engine was thrifty, using only about a quart-and-a-half of gas an hour, at 15 knots. They ranged widely as confidence grew, practicing navigation by compass under starlight.

Salaam found himself picking up the slack for Hiza'a far too often. The man liked to lord it as the lead guy, as long that didn't require actual leading. But Salaam made the best of it, and Abdalla Ali finally said they were, "*Tisbah kafya*" (Good enough.)

Their graduation exercise wasn't boat related at all, but a 200-yard night swim from offshore to the docks in full clothing. Salaam managed it easily despite the icy water and still had the energy to help the struggling Hiza'a ashore.

The next morning they put on civilian clothes, lay down behind bags of winter vegetables in an unmarked Bedford produce truck, and made the 126-mile journey down the M51 to west-central Lebanon.

The rest of the Kamal Adwan operatives arrived at Damour in twos and threes over the first five days of January, in nondescript trucks and cars, carrying papers from bribed officials saying they were farm workers.

Damour, ironically named after Damoros the Phoenician god of immortality, was at a fork in the Old Saida Road, just miles from the coast. There was none of the cedar-clad beauty of much of Lebanon. The town part was half-mile sprawl of bullet-pocked stone buildings, guarded north and south by barbed wire and machine-gun nests. The passers-by saw anxious faces peering out from behind curtains.

The training base in the valley between the town and the inland hills, was a military camp of maybe 10 acres, behind a tall fence topped with shiny-fresh barbed wire. A rolled-earth parade-ground the size of a basket-ball court; was flanked on three sides by barracks, a mess hall, and an admin building. Wider out was a firing range with an earthwork berm, and an obstacle-course weaving among scrubby trees, along a stretch of the Bou Damaa Stream. Shot-up vehicles out in the open, including a bus perhaps left over from the slaughter in the town, completed the facilities.

They were met by two muscular men there to help with their fitness, also Mohammed Masameh, who hovered in the background. The trainers said to go to the barracks that could have slept 40 of them and stake out a cot. Then get food in the mess hall and await instruction. Some knew each other from roadblocks and other duties. Those who recognized Masameh nodded with respect and kept their distance.

Dalal was the last arrival other than Salaam and Hiza'a. Jihad had allowed her a little extra time to say goodbye to her family. Hussain, who'd been a friend at Dbaiyeh, greeted her with pecks on both cheeks. She startled the religious men, Ahmed and Wael, and to a lesser extent Rami, Khaled and Fayadh They weren't used to a woman being among them, let alone with an uncovered head, being treated as an equal. Hussain's warmth toward her raised their hackles even more.

She'd been through these campaigns of whispers and scornful looks before, and knew what had to be done. So did Masameh. He kept her in his sights in anticipation. She left her kit on a cot in the middle of others already in use and headed to the mess for something to eat.

Ahmed and Khaled were carrying plates when she passed them near the serving counter, close enough to hear Ahmed murmur, "*Eahira*" (whore.)

Dalal grabbed a metal tray, wheeled, and smashed it against the back of Ahmed's head. Then put her full force into kicking him as he lay dazed on the floor, punctuating each thud of her boot, with, "Do not... Speak... Of me... That way!"

Dalal understood that respect was made up of equal parts; rapport, admiration, and fear. She couldn't immediately have the first two, so was starting with the last.

She strolled to the counter and got some steaming rice and vegetables, and went to a corner to eat, chewing slowly and deliberately.

Ahmed got up and staggered to the toilet to clean himself up.

No one else acknowledged a thing.

At 10.00 p.m., Masameh had one of his helpers order them to the classroom building. When he entered, they visibly tensed. He was handsome with his wild hair, ragged beard, and muscular body, but daunting with his powerful eyes. Expressionlessly, he said, "You will call me *Baba'a* (Father) and I will punish you like children if you don't carry out my orders instantly and exactly. If you persist in failing me, I will kill you."

No-one complained. They respected that kind of toughness. They would need it during the weeks-ahead.

Baba'a addressing Dalal as Lieutenant, said another man would join them soon, and they'd be the ranking officers under him. Dalal extended an olive branch by saying she should be called "Sister" instead. There were a few encouraging nods of approval. Baba'a covered some housekeeping and waved them away with a warning the next day would be long and hard.

Everyone used the bathrooms at each end of the bunkhouse. There was no running water, just large washing-bowls. The devout members put down rugs and said their *Tahajjud* prayers to the southeast. All settled in.

Dalal felt a growing acceptance. She intended to build on the stand she'd taken with determination and professionalism. At least now, anyone who resented her knew to keep it to himself.
And when she heard the rhythmical rustling of hands under the covers that night and on many nights to come, she smiled and kept that to herself in turn.

NINE

Damour

Breakfast was delivered by their live-in cook, an obsequious Muslim-café-owner survivor of the ethnic cleansing in the town. Following that they drew supplies. Boots and changes of fatigues. Cheap civilian clothing for blending in with the population when outside camp. Canteens, utensils, and personal supplies, all in Chinese packaging. Each got a plastic backpack for their ammunition and other tools.

Their personal weapon was an initially grease-encrusted Czech-made, Kalashnikov AKM fully automatic assault-rifle. An upgraded version of the Chinese AK-47 they were used to. They were told to keep it loaded and at hand's reach at all times. Then their daily training routine began.

There were no easy days. They were up when the sun crested the town, had food, then attended to camp-duties. When the barracks was spotless, there was fitness training. Everyone was in reasonable shape, and could soon complete the obstacle course in decent time. Hiza'a and Salaam, sharpened by their days of boat handling at Latakia, also came quickly up-to-pace.

Early afternoons were for personal weapons training. Then retraining. And training some more. Hours at the range, which reeked constantly of Pyroxylin bullet-propellant. The AKMs had a new firing-lever option for 3-shot bursts. Soon they had the hang of it in all modes. Dalal was good, having qualified during her Lieutenant's training. Jalal, Ramz, and the big and steady Khaled were excellent. Rami was in a whole other class, whether left or right-handed. The only snags were frequent jams from the poor-quality Chinese ammunition. Baba'a promised to get something more reliable.

Dalal marveled at how childishly the men were with their toys. Muslim children are taught that overt gestures, such as high-fives, are bad-manners. These men constantly catcalled, hooted and cheered. She realized that was exactly what they were. Little boys. *Very dangerous little boys.*

The only visible friction was over prayer. Hussain, Ahmed, and Wael were used to the regular ritual. *Fajr* at the first white light of morning. *Dhur* at noon. *Asr,* when a thing's shadow was the same length as its height. *Maghrib* at sunset, *Isha'a* at around midnight. And Tahajjud, any time. Baba'a tackled them about it. From then on, they caught up when they could.

But there were undercurrents. Some fitted in less well than others. All resented Fayadh for his untidiness and ducking of duties. Ramz and Jalal were aloof and anti-social brutes. Tariq spewed politics and hate to anyone he could corner, which soon was no-one.

Hiza'a was a larger problem. His reputation as a fool had caught up with him. It was unlikely the others would follow him into battle. Baba'a decided to discuss it with Jihad at the first chance.

Guest instructors began coming in to teach heavier weapons skills. First the Chinese Type 69 rocket-launcher, which fired a 9lb grenade about 200 yards. Jalal, Ramz, and Rami could already hit a 55-gallon oil drum at 100 yards. Soon everyone was as accurate, first with inert practice rounds, and then with warheads that shredded the thick steel like paper.

Then the Kalashnikov RPK light machine-gun, which had many parts interchangeable with the AKM, but a longer barrel, a bi-pod, and a 75-round drum-magazine. Soon all could pour belts of accurate rounds into the berm at the range.

They also practiced with Russian-made hand-grenades. Dark-gray globes about a pound in weight, designed to fragment and devastate everything within a 10-yard radius. Carrying them loose in backpacks was dangerous. They all got webbing-vests to clip them to.

There were three weapons they would likely run into in Israel. The lightweight, fast firing Uzi 9mm submachine gun, the .223 caliber Galil assault rifle, and the Colt M16 carbine in the same caliber. They learned to strip, reassemble, and fire all three, in case they seized and had to use one.

Ahmed and Wael trained with Semtex explosive, which smelled like almonds, came in 1lb plastic-wrapped blocks, and could be molded by hand like builder's putty. They practiced with different fuse-lengths and learned how to make booby-traps.

Several sessions included the old vehicles, particularly the bus. At the end they knew how to morning, back each other up; in stopping, boarding, clearing and reloading passengers as hostages. You never knew what you might have to do,

When Baba'a decided their weapons-skills were up to speed, they began training from the chin upward. Fatah was one of the first armed groups in the Middle East to train its troops in psychological and ideological warfare.

Jihad had seen its effectiveness during a North Korean visit, including a demonstration right out of the 'Manchurian Candidate.' Members including Baba'a had been indoctrinated in Communist parts of Asia and behind the Iron Curtain. In turn members of the IRA, Red Brigades, and Japanese Red Army, had learned their evil justification in Fatah camps. JRA members had carried out a very successful massacre at Tel Aviv's Lod Airport in 1972.

But Baba'a didn't have the mesmerizing personality needed. For that Jihad provided a stubby, chain-smoking, repulsively toad-faced, 48-year-old Frenchwoman named Shezia Heinrich-Mamatow. The former political science professor and close associate of French anarchist, 'Danny the Red,' had been fired from her tenure at the Sorbonne, after the 1968 Paris riots. Since then she'd been hanging out on the fringes of the Middle Eastern conflicts and was glad of the work. She arrived regally each afternoon in the back of a chauffeured, black Citroën DS21.

Heinrich-Mamatow entered the first session wrapped in cigarette smoke. She had arms-full of materials she unloaded onto two empty desks. Old copies of the PLO newspaper, 'Our Palestine, the Call to Life,' with Jihad's portrait front and center. The Syrian Progressive Front's 'National Covenant.' Articles by and about terrorist leaders Dr. George Habash of Leila Khaled's PFLP, and Nayef

Hawatmeh of the DFLP. Also, Arabic translations of Castro, Guevara, Chairman Mao, Vietnam's Ho Chi Minh and General Giap. Even excerpts from 'Mein Kampf'. The group's wannabe intellectual, Tariq's, eyes lit up.

She plomped an ashtray and two blue packs of Gitanes down on the desk that served as a podium. Surveyed the group while tapping out a fresh one and lighting up. Took a large drag before expelling the smoke off to her left. Then slapped her hand down crack on the desk. "The point of terrorism," she shouted, "Is to frighten people out of their minds!" Jabbing a fat finger, demanded to know what caused the greatest fear in victims. Not waiting, she snarled, "Threats to their children!" Another one of her trademark slaps.

Over and over, and over again, she drove home that uncertainty creates fear, hostages must never have information of any kind. That heightened uncertainty and physical abuse and humiliation increased it. Hostages must not be allowed to use toilets or even stand and stretch. Nor comb their hair, or wash, or apply makeup. Their self-confidence, esteem, and sense of identity must be broken down at all costs.

"Choose one that stands out and make an example! Be brutal. It will keep the others in line, I promise you!"

She knew her topics intimately and argued them compellingly, two hours a day and often longer, six days a week. She preached Marxist-Leninism, Imperialism and the Arab Reaction. Revolution and Counter Revolution; all against a backdrop of Islamic history, the displaced-Arab cause, and evil Zionism.

Heinrich-Mamatow repeated one statement many times. "Terror must terrify! Making people half afraid means nothing! They must be certain their lives are in danger! Then they never forget!"

At the end of a solid three weeks, every operative was in peak condition. Baba'a dialed down the physical activity into maintenance mode. Just an hour of calisthenics morning and evening, and a circuit of the obstacle course. Every other day there was a session on the firing range with all the weapons. Mental conditioning, however, continued daily for as long as they remained at Damour.

TEN

Yarmouk

"So how do you think that helps us, Mr. Spymaster?" Jihad sneered from the comfortable chair in his office on February 2nd.

Iyad was aghast. And mystified by this response to the great news he'd just delivered. He'd thought his boss would be elated. Egyptian-Israeli talks had gone badly, therefore brilliantly for the displaced-Arab cause.

"Khalil perhaps I wasn't clear. President Carter has tilted massively in OUR direction. God knows why. His Jewish supporters must be going nuts."

"And they call this the 'Aswan Formula'?'"

"Yes. Any formal peace treaty ratified by the U.S. must include the two things we want most. Israel pulling back to pre-1967 borders, and a 'Palestinian' solution.' That's tremendous news!"

Jihad was slouched in his seat, palms together in front of his chin. And he never slouched.

Iyad asked, "Look, this is what you wanted, right?"

"Maybe. Maybe. What about these problems Sadat is having with the press?"

"The Egyptian media has turned on him like a nest of cobras. They say he's selling us out too cheaply. That has to be even better for us!"

"Perhaps." Jihad sank even lower. "What is Sadat's response?"

"Trying to appear much tougher at the moment. But never mind him. It's all on Israel's shoulders. What can Begin say? He has to move in our direction."

"It bothers me that Begin and Sadat are even having dinners together," Jihad said morosely.

Iyad shook his head slowly. *Unfathomable. This is more progress toward our own homeland than our entire three decades of fighting has achieved.*

Still, he kept his voice level. "This is an unprecedented opportunity. Powerful forces are aligned in our favor."

"But the Egyptians have pulled their delegations from the Political Committee Meetings, right? I suppose that's something,"

Something? What does the man want?

"That's temporary I think. To take the pressure off Sadat. But all other signs favor us."

"Favor?" Jihad stared at the center of the table as if it was a pit he was considering throwing himself into.

Iyad threw his hands wide. "Yes favor! Khalil I don't understand. We are on the brink here. Our homeland is in reach. All we need is Begin to say yes! Are you so afraid he will say no, that you don't want to raise your hopes?"

Jihad stared at his friend of 18 years as if he were a complete stranger.

Is he such a fool? We've been building up Fatah since, what, 1959? All these years! It's the reason for our existence! Or is he so naïve he can't see what all this means? If Egypt and Israel make peace, it's the end of everything? No more Fatah. No more power!

Operation Kamal Adwan was no longer just about derailing peace talks. It was now about everything.

Jihad had been receiving regular progress reports from Baba'a via Zrayir, that in the main, the trainees were pulling together. But now that the operation was all-consuming, he needed to see that first-hand. Within the hour he and Iyad were on the way to Damour in a gray Mercedes Benz touring car book-ended by fighter-filled technicals. Zrayir was to meet them there. Baba'a had been alerted by a runner from the town, to have the operatives waiting in the classroom. It was a dangerous venture in daylight, but Jihad wouldn't hear of a delay.

He swept into the class-room theatrically, in his tailored black suit and what he fondly believed was a stylish mustard power tie. Iyad was in similar, but better coordinated, gray garb. Zrayir wore his flamboyant Bedouin robe. Jihad started right in.

"I have chosen each of you for the mission of attacking Yáfa from the sea. That is why you've been training in boating, sea navigation, and urban assault. You are here because of your special talents and because the organization has trust in you." He swiveled his head while pausing for effect. Annoyingly, no-one seemed surprised.

Hiza'a has told them this. The man is incapable of keeping anything to himself!

They all gathered around a large table in the corner. Alongside the operatives, the terrorist leaders seemed insignificant. Iyad unrolled some topographical maps he'd brought with them. Jihad detailed the operation as much as was possible so far.

"You'll be in two teams, each in your own zodiac boat." He pointed out where they'd probably launch from the mother ship, and where they would aim for. "Comrade Hiza'a will be overall sea captain responsible for getting you ashore, and will command one team. Sister Dalal the other. I will decide the breakdown of the teams after your final sea training."

Hiza'a's mention prompted some negative expressions.

Important points of reference, like lighthouses and the famous clock tower above Jaffa harbor south of the landing area, were pointed out.

Dalal asked, "And the exact target?"

Jihad's finger moved to an area around Hayarkon Street and Ben Gurion Boulevard, and circled a cluster of hotels, including the enormous Dan Beach Hotel. "Probably one of... these! I will confirm closer to the time."

He brought Salaam into the mix and let him point out places he remembered. Markets, major roads, and features north of the hotels. Enough to be sure they wouldn't be going in blind.

Hiza'a was the one who addressed the elephant in the room. "What will be our escape plan?" Every operative's eyes were on their leaders.

Jihad lied glibly. "You will trade the hostages you will have seized, for a more manageable group of foreign diplomats. Then trade those for our jailed compatriots and air transport to freedom." He pressed the fantasy home with, "Allah willing, we will close off the streets of Yáfa. We might take 500 hostages. Five hundred Jews at gunpoint until our demands are met. They will bargain then!"

He put his hands on the table in emphasis. It wasn't level on its legs and wobbled, adding some slapstick, but he still saw heads nodding.

"At any moment we can destroy everyone! Blow them up in their buildings, no matter how many there are. Our dagger will be a poisoned dagger in the Jews' hearts. If they don't do what we demand, we will take down as many as possible!"

I have them now!

Jihad closed the meeting on that high point, and congratulating them on their hard work so far, about which he'd heard, "Only good things."

It was another lie. He knew from Baba'a there were problems and it was time to find out what they were.

The visitors and Baba'a went to a private area. Baba'a spoke in English. He'd had a Jesuit-Catholic upbringing. Jihad liked to practice his own when he could.

"Sister Dalal has done everything and more. She has the respect of her comrades for her 'follow me or don't, it's your choice' attitude. She backs it up with competence, and they follow."

"Very good."

"But it's the opposite with Hiza'a. He can do the work and did well enough in boat training. But he wants to be liked too much, takes nothing seriously, and is just... not a leader. If we were larger, he might make a useful second-in-command to someone else. But that's not our structure."

"What is our alternative?"

"I would have said Tariq, but he thinks he's cleverer than is the case. Or Rami, but he is a lone wolf by nature. A fearsome wolf, but still a loner."

"How are the rest doing in general?"

"Okay. Salaam likes to dress the part a bit much. Wears webbing with grenades even when others are lying around in tee-shirts. Tariq, Fayadh, Ahmed, and Hussain have taken Ms. Heinrich-Mamatow's teachings to heart. They have a discussion-group. But the experienced ones have proven their worth. Jalal and Ramz scare even me sometimes. The others are performing up to their lesser potential."

"And Allah's sincerer followers?"

Hussain, Wael, and Ahmed, and others sometimes; meet for prayers."

"So, you believe they are ready for the final test?" Jihad asked.

"Yes." Baba'a said. "It is the only way to be sure. It may answer our other questions too."

"Then I will arrange it ."

Jihad left Damour encouraged in some ways, but troubled in others. He saw a decision looming he not want to make.

ELEVEN

Damour

On the following Sunday evening, February 5th, an unusual event happened just as the operatives were bunking down. A canvas-sided truck came down the access road from town. Baba'a's assistants ran to the gate and let it in.

First to climb down were eight bearded, filthy, and stinking Fatah fighters. Rami, Ahmed, Hussain, Jalal, Ramz, Wael, Dalal, Salaam, Hiza'a, Fayadh, Khaled and Tariq, followed by Baba'a and assistants, came out of the barracks to investigate.

Jalal and Rami knew several of the arriving men and called out friendly greetings. They were ignored. With a lot of shouting and the thrusting of gun muzzles, a group of captives were forced down after them.

There were 18 prisoners, both male and female, of a broad age-range. Eight were middle-aged or older. Two men had priest's collars. Three of the women wore nun's habits. They'd been badly abused, from the bleeding faces and obvious pain getting around. One elderly priest had his nose smashed flat. The remainder were teen-aged and younger, down to a girl around seven. All seemed confused, fearful, and stared around wildly.

Baba'a told the operatives to put on their work clothes and boots, and gather their AKMs. While they went about it, it occurred to several there might be a connection to another event that day.

A dusk a yellow earth-moving machine had trundled down from where it had been repairing town roads. It was now parked by the berm at the back of the firing range, under an array of arc-lights.

When everyone was dressed, Baba'a entered the barracks also fully armed, and stood with his back against the closed door. In a menace-dripping voice he said, "Did you think, that you would just, wave your guns at the Jews and they would give you what you wanted?"

His eyes sped from face to face, judging reactions.

"Did you think, their women and children would simply line up to be bargained for? That the Zionists would say, 'But of course you can have your olive groves back. Here! Have this piece of land we stole from you and build yourself a fine house!'"

Baba'a made an expressive motion with his free arm.

"No! These *kāfirs* (unbelievers) were captured today in a house of their God in Chiyah." He meant a Christian suburb of Beirut close to the Green-line.

He stared balefully at Ahmed, Wael and Hussain, the religious ones standing together.

"I was raised with their God. They themselves say his will is un-knowable. Perhaps he has a plan here. That is between him and them."

To everyone he said, "Fatah and Allah's plan is that you will show us you are worthy of the mission that has been given you! Now follow me to the firing range!"

As the operatives walked by starlight and a quarter-moon toward the floodlit distance, with the captives being driven ahead by blows and shouts, each operative confronted his situation. Stomachs churned in some. Bile burned in others. Blind commitment in the abstract, and flying on the wings of a great adventure, were one thing. Mass murder to show their dedication was quite something else.

For those to whom Shezia Heinrich-Mamatow's statements about inducing fear in hostages, and execution as motivation, had been only words; they had become stark reality. A line was about to be crossed. All knew it was a test they must pass .

At the berm, the captives were forced into a huddle within a pool of light. Baba'a gave a command, and a nun was shoved to where he was standing. She blinked confusedly. Baba'a drew his Makarov pistol and shot her in the side of the head. Then leaned over and fired a second shot into her upturned face.

No orders were given or needed. Two more victims were shoved forward, young girls this time. Jalal marched forward and unloaded his AKM on full-automatic into their bodies at a one-foot range. The bullets ripped bloody dirt into the air from the mound behind. Baba'a again applied the coup de grâce.

The bloody-faced priest was next, a set of rosary beads to his lips, muttering in Latin. Rami made to step forward. Baba'a waved him back, and pointed at Wael, who approached confidently enough, but then doubled over and vomited.

Baba'a shouted and when that had no effect, pulled the youth roughly upright and made him lift his weapon. Wael blindly pulled the trigger and missed, but corrected and sent the man down shrieking, to be silenced by Baba'a. Wael lurched away coughing into the darkness.

This went on for ten more minutes.

The third nun tried to stop two young people being separated out and was murdered in their place. Otherwise the captives went to their deaths numbly, realizing there was no hope. The operatives waiting to do their work, knowing Baba'a's glittering eyes were on them.

Rami, Ahmed, Khaled, and Hussain did as they were told perfunctorily, and walked away impassively. Baba'a was always there with his pistol.

Dalal also. Shooting one of the adult men. Ramz sprayed two prisoners with automatic fire where they huddled and finishing the job with single shots to the head with no compunction at all.

Salaam, however, missed his victim with his first two attempts, and then kept the trigger pressed until his gun was empty. Tariq, for all his firebrand revolutionary talk, was nearly as useless. Likewise, Fayadh.

Finally, Hiza'a proved all suspicions correct when his big talk deserted him. Unable to step forward until shouted at, he then couldn't hold his weapon steady. After clumsily completing his task, he too stumbled off retching.

As the group straggled back to the bunkhouse, the earth-mover growled to life, ensuring no evidence would remain come daylight.

Baba'a was thoughtful in his bunk that night.

Yes, some performed well, but enough did not to expose a real risk, that the operation might fail for lack of resolve. I must let Jihad know as soon as possible. Something must be done to shore things up.

"Our training here is finished," Baba'a said to the operatives sitting on cots or leaning against walls around the barracks the next morning.

Few had attended breakfast, and most seemed subdued.

"There is more to be done, but not at this place," he added. "You may have a ten-day leave to do as you wish. Transport will take you wherever you choose. Not all at once, but over the next days. But you must tell the nearest Fatah commander where you are at all times and be ready to rejoin the operation immediately when called upon."

Not everyone took advantage of the opportunity.

Big Khaled, Fayadh who was almost as disliked as Hiza'a, Tariq with his nose in his books on armed struggle, the taciturn Ramz, and brutal Jalal; who to the best of anyone's knowledge had never had a friend, and it was doubtful he'd even had parents; were content to stay in camp.

Of those who did, Salaam wanted to be anywhere else and find himself a woman. He requested passage to Tripoli. Dalal wanted to spend time with her family in Beirut. Hussain, Rami, Ahmed, and Wael wished to go to Shatila to spend time at the mosque on the square. Hiza'a wanted to go anywhere he could impress someone.

Those staying were glad to see Hiza'a go. They were heartily sick of his affecting airs from old

American movies, though he wasn't clowning so much at this moment.

Those leaving took everything with them, including their personal weapon. As they were packing, Baba'a advised them curtly, "You are not to say anything about this operation to anyone, even family or lovers. Anyone who does will be delivered to Azmi Zrayir as a traitor, for his punishment."

On Tuesday morning, leaving his staff to cater for those remaining, Baba'a climbed aboard his own transport bound for Syria.

TWELVE

Yarmouk

That same day, Jihad sat through another of Iyad's briefings on Middle Eastern events. The pendulum had against him. Sadat had been in the US talking with Carter, and had published in the Miami Herald, a reassuring open-letter to the American Jewish community. Those efforts had restarted the joint committee meetings. One between generals had just gone well for Israel in Cairo.

Not that everything pointed toward inevitable peace. The U.S. was angry. A radical Zionist group called the *Gush Emunim* (Bloc of the Faithful,) was breaking ground for an illegal settlement near the archaeologically important city of Shiloh. West Bank passions were ugly, which meant the UN was in an uproar.

Nonetheless, America was acting like any great power, offering the customary bribes. Weapons.

Warplanes in fact. McDonnell Douglas F15s and General Dynamics F16s to Israel and Saudi Arabia. Much-lesser performing Northrup F5s to Egypt, so as not to tip the strategic balance. Fatah would soon have to go cap-in-hand to the Soviets for the latest missiles to counter them.

All of which was troubling at a war-planning level, but not as infuriating as the trouble Jihad was having, finding a mother-ship for 'Kamal Adwan.' He was back on the phone right after the briefing, abusing his envoys in Beirut for their lack of progress.

The problem stemmed from his 1975 attack on the Savoy Hotel in Tel Aviv. That one had also used Zodiac boats launched from a coastal freighter. The freighter been captured afterward by the Israeli navy. The crew was doing indefinite hard-time in Ashkelon Military Prison. That was well known to the Lebanese ship-owning community. Few wanted to take that risk.

Then his phone jingled.

"Yes?"

"*As-Salamu Alaykum* (Peace be upon you.) We have a possible vessel. Not new, but sound. A gasoline-diesel-trader that services the marinas along the coast. Spot diesel prices are high, so it is laid up in basin three, quay 11 of the fishing wharves. The owners will want too much money, but are sensible enough to look the other way."

"Allah be praised. Well done. I will have it looked at."

Jihad received back a skimpy report by nightfall. She was the *Sansato*, meaning 'Sensible,' and seemed far better than that. One hundred feet at the waterline, with a draft of 12. A near-new 550hp diesel motor, which gave her a cruising-speed of over 10 knots. A swing-boom hoist that should be ideal for launching small boats. Accommodation was adequate in a two eight-bunk cabins. Even her color-scheme was right; a black hull and gray superstructure that would make her almost invisible at night with her running-lights doused. The owners were asking an exorbitant $5,000 American dollars a week with no crew.

He hired her immediately for a month, with a promise to return her to her owners, at her home port of Larnaca, Cyprus.

At last he could concentrate on the final three hurdles. The first was finalizing the mission timing, and time was short.

It was the 7th of February, and the two alternate strike-dates he had in mind were the Friday nights of the 3rd and 10th of March. He wanted the operatives to come ashore at sunset as the Jewish Shabbat was beginning. Iyad had assured him street-traffic should be at its lightest. Many workers would have gone home early to their families. To light candles, bless unleavened bread, and share the *Aruchat Shabbat* sacred meal served on the family's finest crockery, over the *Mapah Lavanah* traditional white tablecloth.

He'd need to set one or the other in stone soon, in aid of Zrayir's logistics.

The second was a safe place for the final phase of training. Baba'a wanted one more solid week of hands-on boat exercises. Iyad had suggested a safe-house at the Fatah-controlled fishing village of Es Saksakiye, 40 miles south of Beirut. There was a nearby marina, a training-beach for the Zodiacs and a wharf able to berth a coastal-size ship. The place had hosted clandestine missions before, but not recently. Importantly, it was far enough from the border that if the operatives moved in quietly, and kept themselves invisible by training only at night, they should be safe enough from the American U2 overflights out of Incirlik, Turkey. They would still need to take extreme care.

The final challenge was whom would lead the second team since Hiza'a had proved his uselessness. Jihad needed Masameh's further advice on that.

David Calder

Baba'a arrived in Damascus on an unseasonably bright and warm Wednesday. His Tuesday night had been spent in the tent of a big-breasted, white-blond German archaeological student, at the Joub Jannine Neolithic diggings in the Bekaa Valley.

He'd been full of doubt, questioning his self-worth, and feeling an overwhelming sense of mortality, as he lay in her camp bed with her tracing the scars of wounds accumulated over his 12 years in the struggle. Not even her skilled bringing, of the fine warrior of her overseas study-break, to yet another shuddering climax; dispelled those feelings.

By late afternoon he was in Jihad's upstairs office, with the ever-attentive Iyad also at the table.

Jihad's mood was exuberant from having found his ship. It quickly soured as Baba'a described the teams' status, and the operatives' performance. Or non.

"I still think they will do the work. But with only Sister Dalal to drive them, they'll need to stay in one group."

"Out of the question," groused Jihad. "We've been lucky in the past getting single-teams ashore, but we can't depend on that forever. Besides, the objective requires a pincer approach. There are two entrances on different streets."

"You asked for my opinion," Baba'a huffed, "There it is."

"I know. I know," Jihad placated.

He looked at Baba'a with very mixed feelings. All the operation needed now was determination, and a little luck. In one sense he could appoint almost anyone to make up two the teams. He was sending them to their deaths, after all; you couldn't be too picky. But the better you planned and the better your people were, the luckier you got. A cliché, but still...

This tall, powerful man represented their best chance. But losing Baba'a's skills would be catastrophic for Fatah, and for Jihad personally.

Where will I find another like him?

Still, the operation was his greatest masterpiece.

What choice do I have?

"Mohammed, I need to call on you for something more," he said carefully.

"I know," said Baba'a.

"You do?"

"Yes. I have thought it through. I want to do it."

"You... know the risks?" Jihad dismissed those words immediately with a flick of his hand. "No. We have been comrades too long. You know the almost certain outcome?"

"Khalil, I'm not one of the children you've sent me many times to make ready for the fight. I have fought in your ranks for many years, and sent many men to their death on your behalf, heads full of dreams of the homeland to come. Of regaining our green fields. Our mountains. Our homes."

Baba'a studied his maimed hand for a few moments.

"It's time I struck a blow myself, or I am nothing but a *munafiq* (hypocrite). I must do my part. Myself."

Jihad looked at Masameh with ineffable sadness. "I don't know how I will bear to lose you. And I have never said that to another man."

"It shall be as Allah wills, and as you know I am not a religious man."

Jihad stared out the window at the far, sun-soaked hills, struggling with unfamiliar feelings, then dismissed the moment of weakness.

"Yes it shall."

THIRTEEN

Lebanon

The moment the ship was theirs, Jihad's same envoys started scouring the labor exchanges and hangouts near the Beirut docks for a crew.

The shipping trade had been almost unaffected by the war, in fact was under Fatah's protection because they received most of their armaments that way. There were plenty of itinerant sailors about. The envoys weren't looking for the best men available, just a captain qualified enough to satisfy the Beirut Harbormaster, and a crew certain to keep their mouths shut.

On the 10th, off Ibn Sina Avenue and then a food and trinket stall crowded alley smelling of fish and sweaty humanity, in a Turkish-themed basement bar called Imra Hayakech, they asked the barman to point out a purported ship's master named Karem Osman. The 46-year-old Turk was in a back room acrid with cigarette smoke, playing *Pişti,* a card game similar to 'Snap,' for one Lebanese pound a point.

Osman was a slovenly man, a heavy smoker, with a big belly under a greasy tee shirt, a comb-over, and short stubble covering his entire throat. But he was at least able to show them a current captain's-ticket.

Over strong coffee for the Fatah men, and glasses of milky-colored *Raki* for the Turk, they felt him out enough to decide he could be trusted to keep quiet. Then offered him a generous sum for a couple-of-weeks work dropping spies off the coast of Israel.

After seeing the Sansato from the dock, Osman assured them he could get her underway on two days' notice. Also provide an equally discreet engineer and some deckhands.

A $2000 down-payment changed hands at Rami's old dockside base at Sahet al Najmeh. Osman was promised the same amount when the ship departed Lebanese waters with the 'spies' on board. A half dozen conspicuously armed Fatah fighters were present, to show the consequences of reneging, or telling anyone about the arrangement.

Transport began quietly gathering up the operatives from locations around North Lebanon at the start of the following week. Refreshed and eager, they were literally waiting at their front doors. They had all reached their final training location at Es Saksakiye on the south coast, by Friday the 17th.

The base was on the northwest fringe of town, set back in some trees away from prying eyes, beside a gravel road that transected the coastal highway and ended at the Marina. Behind the house, under a tarpaulin, was a black Datsun pickup truck for shuttling them and their seafaring gear the 500 yards to and from. Their equipment was already inside, including the two deflated Zodiacs. Each arrival drew a sleeping bag and mattress from an equipment room and staked out floor space where they could find it.

"We will be here at least two weeks, so make the best of it," Baba'a said. "The Fatah forces in the town are unaware why we are here. Let's keep it that way. The Jews have spies above, so don't show yourselves or any equipment outside during daylight. Stay fit. Keep your equipment clean. Food will be delivered and we'll cook for ourselves. We will have boating training after dark, every night until we have it right."

Jihad and his entourage soon arrived once again with maps and other props. The operatives were waiting cross-legged in the sparsely furnished lounge.

"Brothers and sister I have important news, and further details of your mission."

He nodded at Iyad, who knew nothing about this news.

"Our intelligence says the Zionists may be better prepared than we thought, and the journey by sea more difficult. So we must strengthen the operation. Comrade Baba'a will join you. He will be in overall command while on the ship. He will also be an equal commander with Sister Dalal when on land. Our strongest seaman Comrade Hiza'a, will be our navigator at sea and guide you ashore."

Salaam knew the best seaman was himself. He might have reacted badly to the insult. Instead he shed a sigh of relief at no longer having to follow Hiza'a's orders. Hiza'a was flattered by the compliment and a little relieved too. He said nothing either. The others murmured approval. Their chances of survival had just soared.

Jihad confirmed his preferred date of March 3rd. That gave them 11 days to complete boat training, then board the Sansato on the 1st, launch boats off Israel on the night of the 2nd, and strike at the planned time of 7:00 p.m. on the Shabbat eve.

"We must attack before the pig Begin travels to Washington in early March. Israel's vulnerability must be first in his mind when he meets with the American Carter!"

The Sansato would drop them off well before dawn, 25 miles off Tel Aviv, to give the ship time to escape toward Cyprus before daylight. They'd need to bide their time before heading to shore. Twenty-five miles was only about four hours motoring in the Zodiacs.

"You will be safe enough unless an Israeli gunboat finds you accidentally. Your small boats will be invisible to their radar."

"If one does?" Fayadh ventured.

"Then you will fight!" replied Jihad, with his trademark punch into one palm.

Lighthouses north and south would position them for the run into the Tel Aviv beach-front. If possible, they were to booby-trap the Zodiacs before making a 200-yard rush inland. During that charge across the sand, they were to kill every Jew they saw. The distinctive Dan Beach Hotel occupied an entire block bounded by Hayarkon Street. Moshe Lahat Boulevard, and Frishman Street. Salaam said he knew the location, but Jihad gave him photographs anyway in case the skyline had changed. Their secondary target would be any heavily populated building, but they were to avoid the ferociously guarded U.S. Embassy, which also stretched between Moshe Lahat and Hayarkon, just to the south.

The assault on the main target would require boldness and good timing. One team would have to run up Frishman onto Hayarkon and block the lobby entrance. The other would allow time for that, then shoot their way in via the staff entrance on the lower level, killing and herding all before them. There would be no evacuation plan. If they'd survived that long, they made it work, or they died.

Once in control, they would secure the hostages, then demand to exchange them. First for some foreign ambassadors. Then for a list of imprisoned comrades and transport from Sde Dov Airport three miles to the north, to Damascus. If the Jews didn't meet their demands within four hours, the expected time needed to mobilize their forces and get ready to take back the hotel, they were to kill their hostages and commit suicide by standing in threes and detonating grenades against their chests.

No one said a word at this, but when Jihad and his contingent departed, some remained where they were, cloaked in their thoughts for some time, before getting up and going robotically about their bedtime tasks.

FOURTEEN

Es Saksakiye

The operatives spent the following day cleaning weapons and other equipment and meticulously weighed everything on a set of bathroom scales. They also received, in shifts, as much boating instruction from Salaam and Hiza'a as was possible without inflating the Zodiacs. When nightfall closed in completely, they loaded their gear on the pickup for the move to the marina for their first night on the water.

There was confusion for a minute or two, because none of the operatives except Dalal could drive. Her doing it was problematic for the religious ones, so Baba'a took on that duty.

At the shoreline, they broke into their teams. The theoretical crewing and loading, based on skills and weight distribution, had been worked out with the scales.

Dalal and Baba'a would be in the left front of the two boats, and the two best shooters, Jalal and Rami, in the right front. Those two would remain armed in case an Israeli Naval searchlight stabbed out of the darkness. Hiza'a would drive Dalal's Zodiac with five others aboard and Salaam the other with four extras. That allowed for 120lbs of weapons and ammunition down the centerline of Dalal's boat, and 300lbs including the machine-guns and explosives; in Baba'a's. Both boats would still be well under 1650lbs. The plan was to train in that configuration for the next nine consecutive nights.

They launched via davits and a hand-winch at the end of the wharf, onto seas roiled by persistent spring Khamsin winds. All appreciated the comfort and stability of the rubber boats, both in ocean rollers and the nasty inshore chop. Everything seemed practical, flexible and doable. Only arming themselves quickly at sea, in case the need arose, proved trickier than expected. The answer was to stow the dry-bag of less needed equipment underneath, and the weapons bag of AKMs, ready to fire, on top, secured with stretchy cords.

Around 11:00 p.m. they landed on the shelving beach, deflated the boats, packed them and their engines in their tough rubberized carry bags, and like Cinderella's rats, were back at the safe-house before midnight.

During the days, there were always men in corners doing sit-ups, press-ups, or working with weights, competing for the most impressive total in one session. An almost continuous game of *Tarabish*, a Lebanese version of the addictive American game '500,' went on at the kitchen table. Khaled always seemed on the winning team no matter who he partnered, hooting, "I win again!" as he snatched up the winnings. The prayer group at the sacred times grew to include everyone except Dalal, Jalal, Ramz and Baba'a. The newer members followed along or haltingly re-conjured prayer chants from childhood. "... All praise is due to Allah, Lord of the world. The beneficent, the merciful. Master of the Day of Judgment..."

Beirut

Karem Osman had soon found a crew. Greek deckhands, Xavos and Tomaso, and a fellow Turk named Hasan, as ship's engineer. When he took them aboard for a proper inspection, Hasan immediately saw a leak in the Sansato's cooling system. Not a major repair, but he would have to dismount the engine to get at the split pipe. Several days' work.

Iyad told Jihad about this on the 26th, the same day he was fighting a crisis. Their old colleague-in-terrorism, Abu Nidal, had assassinated Egyptian

Cultural Minister Yusef Sibai, one of Sadat's closest friends, in Nicosia. Sadat had retaliated by canceling all displaced-Arab rights-of-residence in Egypt. Already in a rage when the second news came in, Jihad had the envoys who'd first inspected the Sansato, and who'd found Karem Osman, invited into cars on Beirut streets, and shot in fields.

Since there was no chance of changing ships, the operation would have to be delayed a week. The new departure date would be March 9th and the strike date, the 10th.

Iyad had also spoken to the Marina owner in Es Saksakiye. When he explained the plan, the owner pointed out the depth of water beside the marina wharf. Far less than the Sansato needed. The operatives would have to inflate the boats on the beach and motor out to the ship, instead of walking aboard over a gangplank. It meant being exposed, longer than hoped, to the Hawkeye pinpoint cameras aboard the U2s.

But at least the problem had been found in time to adjust.

And at least Iyad's spies were saying things were unchanged in Israel. There was only the usual amount of political white noise. Israel complaining about the U.S. arms sales to its enemies. Ezer Weizman hinting that Israel's air bases in the Sinai were off the peace table. Regular contact between Carter and Begin, but leading to nothing.

The fallback dates, and an attack on the Friday at dusk, looked as good as the originals.

Es Saksakiye

The operatives had been counting down until there would be final prayers and meals, last minute equipment checks, and they'd be on the water, when the news came via Zrayir. The date change threw them off temporarily. For a few days, faces moped and the safe-house stank of cigarettes being chain-smoked to combat the disappointment and boredom. But that passed.

Then on the afternoon of the 8th, the day out from departure, a new tension began building. Around a conversation that was taking place in sexual semaphore, using just the eyes.

Well yes, of course, but how with so many around and no privacy?

I will make a way.

Soon even the slowest knew Sister Dalal wanted Salaam as her lover for her last night in Lebanon. Wael, Fayadh, and Ahmed took their mattresses into other rooms. Salaam was lying on his back when Dalal came in and lay down. She propped on an elbow with a hand flat on his chest, barefoot, wearing a rumpled linen blouse without a bra, and baggy Sherwal trousers with a string for a belt.

She smelled to Salaam of *Katara* shower soap. It made him think of summer in Kashmir's fabled Mughal gardens of Nishat, which he'd heard about on his mother's knee.

He'd bedded many women, but mostly out of competitiveness. He didn't have a strong sex-drive. His craving was much deeper. If a woman desired him, it meant he existed. In fact, he was prudish and shy, and couldn't express his needs even if he knew what they were.

No other encounter had been like this. His forte was teenage city-girls who couldn't keep their hands off him in nightclubs. Their only demands were to lie beside his, to them, beautiful body and let him have his way. Well, perhaps one or two married women had known what they wanted, but never like this. He'd no idea how to respond.

Dalal's doubts and uncertainties were not about fucking. She was naturally adventurous and had taken to sex like a flower to a summer's day, reveling in the primitivity and sweatiness of it all. Celibate since that day at Yarmouk that ended her relationship with Umri. she needed to be taken. But with gentleness also. And acknowledgment, again, for perhaps the last time; that she was a woman.

Salaam put his hand, he thought softy enough, on her bare shoulder. The palm was rough from weeks of hand-over-hands along an obstacle-rope. Dalal flinched. He scraped it along her back under her blouse. She tensed again, but let him explore. He groped her breasts and then reached lower, toward her cleft. She slapped his arm away.

"Don't maul me! You are not playing with your cock now! Don't you know anything?"

Salaam jerked away as if stabbed with a knife. The room went dead and cold. Dalal looked into his awkwardly hanging face. He had full, almost feminine lips, and a nose that wouldn't have shamed Michelangelo's David. The expression was of a guileless boy.

"Here, let me. Lie back."

She took off her cotton top, unbuttoned his shirt and put her hand on his stomach, moving her fingers soothingly. She wondered how a body could be so hard. So arrogantly male.

He writhed and made a soft sound.

Dalal felt the familiar, growing warmth and slickness between her thighs. Her hand circled gradually wider, the bottom edge slipping rhythmically further and further beneath his waistband. Salaam's breathing became ragged.

She separated his buttons and her fingers encircled his warm, hard, pulsing cock, which was thick and pink in the lamplight. She caressed it for a few seconds, enjoying having pure control.

Feeling him shuffle the pillow under his head so he could watch, she smiled. She moved down. His musk filled her nostrils, pungent and sweet at the same time. His taste filled her senses. The taste of... oneness. His hips moving in time with the bobbing of her head.

She tried to prolong, but control had switched. Salaam gripped her hair and groaned from the depths of his belly as he arched. She luxuriating in the joy of the intimate act.

While they cooled, she thought of his powerful hands in her hair. The masterful grip that had been so fulfilling.

Salaam soon stirred, recovering. His fingers played with her hair. Dalal shuddered. Beside her elbow, his maleness twitched as it hardened. She lifted her head to see his eyes.

"Nassarini ana." (Take me!) She said playfully.

Salaam shook his head, not understanding.

"Nassarini ana!"

He pulled her face to his, and they kissed long and hard, sharing tongues. She thrilled knowing he didn't care where her mouth had been, only about possessing her. Her head fell back in ecstasy.

What will he do? Force me to my knees and use me? Wrap my tits around his cock and make me lick while he thrusts?

She loved those English words she'd learned in the camps. So excitingly, deliciously, dirty.

"Sharmuta," he blurted.

Yes, I will be your slut!

He was at her entrance, spreading her wide. She moaned, *"Nekni ana! Nekni ana!"* (Fuck me!)

Salaam lifted her with every delicious thrust, until there was only the taste in her mouth and their scent of their sweat, and the feeling of being stretched ever wider. Their cries soared before trailing away into paralyzed gasps. The lovers subsided to heaving rest.

Dalal was owned. Therefore, she must be worthy.

FIFTEEN

Es Saksakiye

The Sansato announced herself with the rumble of her anchor chain from offshore, which sent seabirds wheeling and screeching above the marina.

The operatives had eradicated all evidence of their presence at the safe-house, and shuttled themselves and their gear down to the water in shifts, a half-hour before. Hiza'a and Salaam were just finishing inflating the second boat with a foot-pump.

A convoy of dimmed-head-lit vehicles pulled up on the road above. Silhouettes of armed men appeared on the skyline. Jihad came down into the fringe of the wharf-lights, and everyone gathered around.

"If anyone wants to withdraw, then say so."

Surprised eyes flickered to the gunmen close by, knowing they'd be taken aside and shot if they spoke up. No one got this deeply into a Fatah operation and walked away. They were fighters in the cause. There never had been any going back.

Jihad handed Baba'a a paper in both Arabic and Hebrew, listing the prisoners he wanted released from Israeli jails. The first name on it was Musa Juma al-Tallka, the lone survivor of the Savoy Hotel attack. Fatah knew he'd died in custody more than a year before. The name was a prop, a suggestion Fatah looked after its own. A blatant lie.

Money for the captain, and a Japanese waterproof watch so Baba'a could keep time aboard ship, changed hands. Also a two-way radio, with a list of frequencies Fatah HQ said they would monitor, taped to the back.

"Fi Amanullah" (May Allah protect you.)

'Insha'Allah," the operatives replied in chorus.

The Zodiacs took the operatives out to the Sansato. Eleven of them scaled a cargo net while Salaam and Hiza'a returned for the dry-bags of weapons. Then the boats were shipped and the cargo net thrown over them as camouflage.

The Sansato grumbled her anchor back aboard, and with dimmed running-lights, gathered momentum on a south-south-westerly heading. Baba'a looked up and acknowledged the bulky shape framed in the wheelhouse window. Then the terrorists took their personal gear and went below to eat the leftovers of their last meal, and get some sleep.

Karem Osman had thought he knew from the beginning, whom he would be taking aboard. Seeing their equipment dispelled any doubt. Spies didn't need the volume or the types of weapons obvious even inside their sealed bags. He knew very well the fate of the ship's crew from the Savoy Operation.

Therefore, he intended to stay far away from any ships of the Israeli navy. Though he didn't know it, in fact nobody did due to a failing of Iyad's spies, there was danger of that at all.

The World Youth Yachting Championships were taking place off Tel Aviv over the next few days. An important event on the Israeli tourism-calendar that warranted every protection. Over the last few hours, the Israeli Navy's VLD radar, on top of Haifa's Mount Carmel, had been watching bad weather develop in the Mediterranean. The IDF were busy moving their ships south for search and rescue duty if needed.

It was overkill then, that during the engine repairs Osman had made Hasan disconnect the ship's speedometer and odometer. If anyone had asked, he'd have said there'd been no time to get them working again.

Logic told him that the leader of these terrorists would know where he was supposed to be dropped off. That was a point 25 nautical miles north and west of Tel Aviv. Roughly 98 miles and 9 hours steaming at the Sansato's regular cruising speed. Just as shrewdly he believed the terrorists, in the dark, would have no way to relate engine pitch to speed and distance.

He planned to motor slowly and on a subtly zigzag course, about 65 miles south to somewhere west-south-west of Haifa, a northernmost city. Also further out to sea so the city lights wouldn't give him away. He even had one other trick in his bag, for covering his treachery.

The captain looked out around them. The sea was calm and visibility fair under a light sea haze. It hadn't registered that there'd been no red sunset. Not that it would have mattered. All Karem Osman cared about was collecting his money and saving his skin.

At 4:00 a.m. there was no-one on deck to see Xavos follow his captain's orders, remove an item from each boat, and dropping them over the side. The deckhand then woke Baba'a and took him to the captain.

Osman pointed to a spot on a chart and said they were about 30 miles off Tel Aviv, on an easterly bearing toward the drop-off point. ETA was half an hour. Baba'a knew no better. He headed back to rouse the others.

Everything about the boats seemed as they'd left them. All they had to do was lift the hulls and lower the motors. But from the way the first Zodiac swung side-to-side when it rose above the railing, there was now a breeze. Baba'a went to the railing and stared out into the darkness. There was a keen wind, and a burgeoning swell.

Despite that, launching into the lee of the ship's tall black hull went like clockwork. Baba'a was the last over the side after paying the captain. Engines pushing strongly, they drew away from the Sansato's in trail formation.

A dome of unbroken darkness had replaced the stars. But the wind was still only about 10 knots, not enough to form whitecaps. Adrenaline levels were so high no one felt vulnerable. While the two-foot swell kept the two boat-captains' hands full, everything seemed to be going well.

Then Hiza'a shouted, echoed by Salaam. The compasses were gone. Behind them in the distance, the Sansato's engine surged as she hastened away toward Cyprus.

Baba'a shouted over the hubbub, "Save your energy! The wind is from the west, so downwind is Palestine. At dawn we will navigate by the sun until we see Yáfa's lighthouses."

The engines were shut down to save fuel. Carry-ropes un-threaded from loops on the hulls and used to tether them together. Oars assembled to keep the convoy headed into the swell.

Baba'a tried radioing Fatah to report their predicament, but chattering Hebrew voices filled all the channels. Sometime in the night, water shorted out the radio and they couldn't get it working again.

Dawn began as a watery glow that soon brightened in all directions, dashing their hopes of using solar-navigation. Full daylight brought a uniform drizzling grayness, blotted out at times by squalls. At least the seas hadn't gotten worse.

Noon came by Baba'a's watch. Everyone was violently seasick. The adrenaline-laced excitement of the launch had long degenerated into dogged misery. Salaam offered snippets of advice. "Drink water!" As if there was an alternative. "Try to keep your eyes off the sea, and on something that doesn't move!" Everything was moving.

Fortunately the Zodiacs dealt with the rugged conditions as comfortably as could be hoped and took aboard remarkably little water. Most of that was rainwater. They drank and saved some and took turns bailing out the rest with a tethered canvas scoop.

By 4:00 p.m. most could keep down some food, but there was obviously no chance of landing in Israel any time soon. With that went their Shabbat-eve attack.

The light faded and left them alone again on the heaving sea.

SIXTEEN

North-West Israel

Fayadh was the first to see one. He'd been woken at daybreak on the Shabbat morning, 50 miles out in the Mediterranean, by what sounded like birds chirping. A shiny snout and a pair of mischievous black eyes rose out of the much-calmer sea to study him. Then the bottle-nosed dolphin chattered to its pod-mates and dived again.

By then the frolicking creatures were all around them, seeming as surprised as the humans. To the inland Arabs especially, they were as magical as unicorns. The pod re-grouped and undulated away. Fayadh shouted, *"Bel hew 'elamh!"* (It is a sign!) Heads agreed, and the steersmen scrambled to start the motors.

But inside a minute the dolphins had vanished. The terrorists carried on anyway, keeping the lightest part of the sky behind them until all directions were equal. Then they plugging on by instinct.

Distant towers appeared through the coastal haze in the early afternoon. The chimneys of the Israeli central-coast, coal-fired power plant at Hadera; not that they had a clue. The shapes dissolved again as the slight Mediterranean tide carried them north. But in a while, white patches broke through the gray and soon became surf beating on beaches and rocky outcrops.

Little was said. Hiza'a and Salaam stoically pointed them at the broadest white area just north of a low headland. There seemed to be buildings beyond that, and a hint of much higher ground farther back.

It was soon clear they were approaching a sandy bay, with an ancient, elongated masonry running parallel to the beach and fragmenting at a stream-mouth. The marvelous remnants of a 2nd century aqueduct built by Hadrian's Romans. To their south were seething dragon-toothed reefs.

Within another minute the engine of Hiza'a's inflatable spluttered to silence They hurriedly tethered the boats again to keep in a group, and Salaam's took over the lead. That got them half the distance to shore before its tank also ran dry. They assembled oars and crept beach-ward.

One hundred yards offshore, Salaam mentioned the lettering on the stream-mouth's blue sign said

'Taninim.' Inland were muddy fields, then the blocky buildings, and unpaved streets and alleys of an Arab town. They hunched instinctively, and would have ducked even lower, if they'd realized they were in full sight of the largest Kibbutz in Israel. Kibbutz Ma'agan Michael, with its many acres of Tilapia ponds. Baba'a knew only one thing. They weren't anywhere near Tel Aviv.

Fifty yards out, the surf started to sweep them in. They un-tethered again and put away the oars except one each boat to steer with. Baba'a ordered the dry bags unzipped to arm themselves for the landing, and there was a commotion on Baba'a's boat. The RPK machine-guns and explosives had been inadvertently put back on top. In the struggle for AKMs and magazines, they neglected to keep the boats straight.

They were abreast on the edge of the white-water, when Salaam freed his weapon and pulled on his grenade-festooned webbing. A breaker gripped and propelled the craft forward like surfboards. All gripped what they could, white-knuckled, with the hand not holding a weapon. The wave rode over a rise in the sea floor, and thrust Baba'a's boat violently upward. Then it flipped.

Everyone on the low side fell out sideways. Wael, Ahmed, and Salaam went up in the air, with Ahmed's flailing AKM-stock crunching against Salaam's head. The weight of his vest; sank him like a stone. The

Zodiac came down on Ahmed, knocking him out or worse, and trapping Wael beneath.

The second Zodiac had beached safely. The occupants hauled their craft free of the waves and rushed to help. Just in time to see Ahmed being carried face down out to sea. They steadied the upturned boat while Khaled ducked beneath. He grabbed Wael's battledress and hauled him out into the open air. They lifted the limp body onto the hull and dragged the hulk ashore.

Dalal was in hysterics, jabbering unintelligibly at the water's edge. Fortunately, the rescuers had gotten to Wael in time. After a few minutes of crude CPR, and him spewing up copious seawater, he was breathing again on his own.

Only then did everyone collapse from exhaustion.

It was 3:42 p.m.

SEVENTEEN

Haifa, Israel

At 7:30 a.m. on the Shabbat morning, members of all ages from the Egged Bus Company's social club for drivers and their families, the *Navads* (Wanderers,) began arriving at the company's Terminal at Bat Galim on the Haifa foreshore, excited about the club's day-excursion. They would be going to the Sorek Stalactite Cave near Beit Shemesh, southeast of Tel Aviv.

Their company-supplied bus waited for them at a passenger island. It was one of the newer 'Intercity' models; registration number 88-191, in Egged's latest red-with-white-trim, color-scheme. The company emblem of Hebrew letters stylized into the wings of the God Mercury, gleamed on the grille.

Egged had imported the chassis from Saab-Scania in Sweden. The passenger-body had been added by the Yochelman Merkavim company in nearby Hadera. They'd done a fine job, using heavy steel framing, thick plywood flooring, and paneling of sixteenth-inch sheet-steel. The wear-areas were overlaid with Formica-veneer, and the 52 seats made of steel tubing, padded with kapok and trimmed in pleasant pastel-shaded plastic. Boarding and disembarking were by concertina-doors front and back.

Wanderers' expeditions were festive events. Unlike their orthodox friends, whom they respected greatly but knew would be happier at home with their *Torahs,* the Wanderers took seriously the holy book's *Oneg Shabbat* (enjoyment of the Sabbath) commandment. It encouraged eating, singing, and joyful times with family and friends.

Mothers had bought bags of toys and clothing changes. Everyone had goodies for a bring-and-share picnic lunch, a lot of it leftovers from the previous night's sacred feast. Every trip they said they'd take less, but always seemed to bring more.

The families, all young to middle aged, included nature-loving Marion and Harel Abadi and their four young-people. Also their hiking-friends Leah and Avner Geffen, enjoying the quickly improving weather with their two young ones.

Other close bonds existed between Lavan and Jacob Horvath, and Sharona and Saul Gerstman, who'd brought along their respective broods. All-together, there were soon eight families-with-children aboard, all chatting excitedly.

The singles and pairs included enormous ex-paratrooper Jethro Dag, without his Dutch wife and children because one was sick. Also Ron Marks and his daughter Moira, and Gabriel Hahn, the day's designated driver, with his wife Judith.

Experience had taught the parents to leave the rear bench-seat clear, for children to color in their books and otherwise amuse themselves. All the other seats were occupied when Gabriel made sure the short curtains bracketing the side windows were open for maximum visibility, then strolled up the aisle slapping seatbacks and announcing he was ready to go. Carry-bags were quickly zipped and stowed. Several babies were given bottles more for their parent's enjoyment that their own.

Gabriel closed the doors and eased the bus out onto Retsif Aharon Rosenfeld Avenue. They turned onto Hubert Humphrey Drive and followed the waterfront anti-clockwise to the onramp to highway 2 south. The 'Coastal Highway' route would hug the Mediterranean all the way to Tel Aviv before swinging inland to skirt the Metroplex. They'd then take via highway 4 to Beit Shemesh, before climbing the Judean foothills to the Sorek Cave.

As they passed Tirat Carmel and the truly open road began, Rivka Beckman, the group's unofficial cheerleader, moved her sons Raviv, 6 and Alon, 3, off her lap. She looked over at her husband Ariel, who preferred 'Ari.'

"Now?"

He grinned, and Rivka got her first song going. Chana Malhina's anthem, '*Yerushalay'm Ba'or*' (Jerusalem in the Light.)

Jerusalem in the light
How warm your stone glows
In early morning and fading light
As my heart glows with you.

Holy City, burning bright
Temple fountains of my heart
O'er Eretz Israel you shine unmatched
To your sacred bosom draw me close.

The Wanderers' tradition of juicing up gentle songs had everyone stomping along.

Taninim

When the terrorists had recovered sufficiently to get up off the sand, they went to the Zodiac to re-arm themselves. And stared in horror. The RPKs and explosives left unsecured during the chaotic landing, were at the bottom of the sea.

The RPKs were no vital loss; their purpose had been to defend a captured mid-city hotel. There were none in sight. And only Ahmed and Wael had trained with the explosives anyway. Ahmed was dead and

Wael in no condition to play with things that blew up. And they had plenty of everything else. Each boat had carried enough Kalashnikovs for everyone, though some were older AK47s distinctive for the foldout bayonet. There was plenty of ammunition and grenades, and the RPGs.

When Rami had locked and cocked, he trotted away to turn the corner at the stream and scout along the far bank of the stream. That was the obviously route to get inland. He passed the sign Salaam had pointed, The Hebrew text jolted home the reality of their situation.

Dalal meanwhile, stayed seated above the high-water mark, watching the sand between her boots. The others thought she was weeping over Salaam Instead a fuming determination had taken hold of her. *At long last I am sitting on MY land. This is MY place, and I will kill anyone who tries to say otherwise.*

For another thing she was fed up with living in Baba'a's shadow. Jihad had appointed her one of the leaders, and lead, was what she was going to do.

Within a minute Rami was back, on one knee hissing, "There is a woman! With a camera!"

This was Dalal's moment. She tucked the Palestinian flag she wore as a scarf, into the vee of her battle-jacket. Rushed to the boat, and seized an AKM. Cocking it on the run, she splashed across the shallow stream-mouth, then crouched and crept slowly. The woman was a hundred yards upstream, face pressed to a Leica 35MM camera fitted with her best close-up lens, facing into a bush on the other bank.

Beth Cohen was an attractive 38-year-old from New York City. As a wildlife photographer she was in her element at Taninim. The nature reserve was one of the last fragments of Israel's coast, still in its natural state. And right after a storm was the perfect time for take photos for her agent back home, where her work featured regularly in prestigious coffee-table magazines. She got the adjustment just right, then sighed as the rare and elusive Waterside Warbler she'd been stalking, hopped to a different twig.

Damn bird! Stay still!

Beth heard legs swishing through wet grass. She turned and stared blankly, until she realized the woman running toward her with the bright-colored and bulky scarf around her neck, was holding a rifle. She glanced frantically about, but there was no help in sight.

Dalal yelled, "Awqif! Awqif!" (Stop! Stop!) though Beth wasn't moving.

It was some command in Arabic, but what? Bethe barely even knew enough Hebrew to get by.

When the women were just feet apart, Dalal launched into demands, not giving Beth time to answer. Then seemed to realize from Beth's jeans and blue windbreaker and the second expensive Leica camera around her neck, she was a westerner, and switched to badly accented English.

"This is Taninim." Beth replied, bewildered. "I am photographing birds. Please!"

"Which way Tel Aviv?"

Beth pointed south down the coast beyond the headland. "There. A long way!"

"Where you from?"

"America. I'm a nature photographer."

"How you get here?"

"I drove. I have a car. Over there!" She pointed at an orange roof showing above some bushes. "Please don't hurt me. Please!"

"No," Dalal shouted, "How you get HERE? To my land! This is MY land not yours!"

"They... they... this is Israel," Beth said abjectly. "I am Jewish. They gave me a visa!"

Dalal's rage erupted. Her AKM's muzzle kicked viciously and sharp reports lashed the broad open space. The American woman as was hit in the torso, and a second time in the upper chest. The third round passed over her shoulder. Beth cried out softly and fell.

Dalal didn't look down, just wheeled and went back to the others. Nothing was said as she went by. The terrorists followed her to the boats, where Wael lay half conscious and coughing, to gather up their deadly equipment.

EIGHTEEN

Israel

Elsewhere during Shabbat morning, Israelis from all parts of society were waking up to an overcast and drizzly day, though lightening skies suggested improvement-to-come.

At a vegetarian *Moshav* (collective community) in the Galilean hills, a musical prodigy practiced clarinet-notes while his family packed suitcases. In Jerusalem a government-representative, who had an extremely famous father, fretted about disappointing a policeman he admired, and over what the outcome would be for national security. Many people, in a small town beside the Coastal Highway, were excited about a Premier League soccer match. Loving couples, one each in Tel Aviv and Hadera, and two in Haifa, plotted afternoon trips along the Coastal Road.

By 2:30 p.m., at Tel Aviv's Neve Sha'anan main bus station in the southern suburbs, people were arriving for travel in the opposite direction from the Wanderers.

One person was full-of-life, Ranya 'Rani' Wolfowitz, a tall and graceful 14-year-old with long brown hair and an impish smile. She couldn't wait to tell her friends of the fashions she'd seen on trendy Dizengoff Street while attending her cousin's Bar Mitzvah, with her mother Chaima.

Another was Miriam Ehrman, 18, ebullient, tomboyish, and about to begin her mandatory two years of IDF national service. She wanted to be a spy. She carried her guitar wherever she went, and that morning had enjoyed the time of her life busking on Old Jaffa's Second Aliyah Wharf.

There was also German-born Mathew Benenson in his business attire, He'd been up early, watching the weather anxiously while laying out shirts on his bed. Now he was worried about the voyage from Haifa by England on a buying trip for his parent's business. He was prone to seasickness. Nothing seemed to help. But then he always worried.

A number were elderly. The bus-driver let those board immediately. Else Shwin and Simcha Cohen were matrons traveling separately. Josef 'Joe' Hallwany, from a line of Rabbis who protected the Cave of Elijah near Damascus, was 66 and proud of his full head of dark hair. He was going home to his night-job at the Talpiot night markets. Ori Swartz was a dignified, barrel-chested man homeward-bound from his grandson's birthday party. The 73-year-old hoped to doze on the bus in the Mediterranean sun. Martha Mizrachi, clutching her carpet-type handbag, and Sapira Lindner, whose many friends, and the family she missed, called her 'Princess.'

Though Haifa was home for most of those traveling, Russian-born carpenter, Daniel Izrailevich, was going home to Acre, and Moshe Abergil was taking a break at his apartment on Mount Carmel, from his stressful sales job. An attractive young couple, Leah Tavor and Gilad Goldstein, held hands and looking enrapturedly into each other's eyes. They were reporting as ordered to Nahariya, for Gilad's ritual family-vetting.

When everyone was settled, two Egged drivers came aboard.

Jericho 'Jeri' Karam, in charge, was a small, jolly, square-faced and curly haired, 34-year-old in black pants with ironed creases, and a starched white shirt.

Dov Dreier, a muscular, premature-balding 46-year-old with an oversized drooping mustache, was a competitive Masters weightlifter in his spare time. Also, one of Egged's most popular tour guides. He was riding-along home to his family in the *Krayot* (townships) north of Haifa. He went straight to the back to doze away a hangover.

Jeri said a hearty "*Nesi'ah Tovah!*" (Let's have a great trip!), let off the air-brakes with a pop-hiss, and drove out of the depot toward the commencement of Highway 2.

It was 2:46 p.m.

Taninim

The problem for the terrorists, right off, was what to do about Wael. He couldn't walk yet. If it were left to Jalal or Ramz or a few others, they would shoot him. Dalal, even in her zeal, wouldn't think of it. Besides that, people alerted by the gunfire were watching from the balconies of the high-rises. They'd been ordered to booby-trapped the boats, but the explosives being lost precluded that, and the scrutiny made them nervous.

They took the best of the Kalashnikovs, clipped grenades to their vests and put more in their backpacks, and gathered as many banana-clips of ammunition as they could carry. Ramz, Ahmed and Jalal each took a grenade launcher and projectiles. After also sharing out Wael's gear. Baba'a assembled a pair of oars, peeled off the man's fatigue-jacket and his own, and they lifted Wael onto the makeshift stretcher. Ramz and Khaled took ends.

But Dalal wasn't done applying her stamp. She made everyone gather in a group, then shouted.

121

"Kamal Adwan," just like in training. "Deir Yassin," the rest responded: the Palestinian war-chant on many battlefields since the Hagenah's massacre at that town during the Nakba.

The murderous group splashed around the corner from the beach and set off along the riverbank toward the highway indicated by the American woman. Feeling naked on the exposed ground beside the sports-fields. Even the right-handed terrorists bore their AKMs pointing toward the town.

As they passed the American woman's car, a sporty little Fiat 850 hatchback, a glance said it was useless to them. Two of them might have gotten in, if one kept his head out the window. There was a small-child's stuffed toy on the passenger's seat, a curiosity later to those who knew Beth Cohen had no children. She had a row of them on her mantelpiece in nearby Caesarea. Ramz smashed the back window spitefully with the butt of his AKM.

The stream-bank became scrubbier and swampier. Wael was trying to sit up, but still wasn't speaking coherently. Baba'a ordered him to be still.

Finally, they came out of the scrub on the south side of a bridge. The Highway was two lanes with a raggedy-grassed divider. A large blue sign had the numeral 2 in white in the center, and the 90 kilometer-an-hour speed limit.

They went back into cover to make a plan.

It was 4.32 p.m.

Kibbutz Ma'agan Michael

A large, disgruntled-looking, highly overdressed man in a dark suit sat at a dusty desk in the corner of packing-shed cluttered with scoop-nets and smelling of fish-food-pellets. He was wielding a yellow highlight-pen over a multi-page official document with the logos of the Israel Knesset, and a minor political party called Coalition for Change. Reserve Army Major General and Knesset member Yuri Dubinsky was two days off his 55th birthday. He'd retreated there to work on an important bill. He'd just turned a page when a kibbutz worker came in to say he'd heard three gunshots.

"It's probably those kids from the Arab village with fireworks or something, but you'd better go look. Take Shem. And Reuvan if you can the lazy bugger. It's his damn job. And an Uzi."

"Yes sir."

Before very long the worker and a companion raced gasping into the packing shed . Dubinsky turned, furious, to see why.

"There are...," said one.

"Boats." said the other.

"Where? What kind?"

"In the bay just this side of the stream," said the first.

"Zodiacs," said the second.

Dubinsky picked up the shed-phone and dialed a number from memory. It rang at an up-scale, five-

123

bedroom unit in Kfar Yona, a dormitory suburb of Tel Aviv. The men were fidgeting.

"Yes?"

"We also heard...," said the first.

"More shooting," said the second.

Then in chorus, "Just now over by the highway!"

But the general had suffered a ruptured eardrum while deputy commander of the tank corps. He'd clapped his hand over his free ear when a deep voice came on the line. He'd missed the last sentences.

General Zamir Aranov, commander of the *Magav* (National Border Police,) said, "Ah Yuri! How are you general?"

"Look Zamir, some of my guys have found boats. Those rubber ones the Arabs use."

"Really? I'll have my people in Haifa get down there right away!"

"I knew you would, so I called you first." Dubinsky noticed his two men still hovering and vigorously shooed them away.

Very good, thought Aranov. *Never miss the opportunity to get one up on the other agencies, especially with the tight budgets these days.*

"Shall I give the local police a call too?"

"No no no. No need to cause a panic. Just keep your people indoors, hey? My boys won't be long!"

Within a minute Dubinsky was back reviewing his document. The Knesset was meeting on the coming Tuesday.

At a nearby accommodation-block, a door opened. Reuvan Erlich, a moon-faced and seriously overweight 40-year-old security guard, emerged from a late lunch with his sister fumbling in his pockets out of habit.

Reuvan had been dying for a fag for more than an hour. He would have killed for a whole pack of Dubek Filters. The nearest shop was at Zichron Ya'akov, on the other side of the pedestrian overbridge. He set off toward Highway 2.

NINETEEN

Beit Shemesh

"Unbelievable!" "Enchanting!' Those were typical comments from the Wanderers as they emerged from the Sorek Limestone Cave. It had been discovered during expansion of a quarry and kept secret for years.

Inside the temperature-controlled labyrinth a tour guide led them along a raised wooden footway, wending among stalactites and mites, past fantastic and color-lit shapes resembling macaroni, fried eggs, an ice-cream cone, Snow White and the Seven Dwarfs; even a realistic lion. Many went back for a second time.

At noon they gathered food, and blankets they spread out in a wild-flower-decorated, natural amphitheater with a spectacular northern view. When children were appeased, they began a Wanderers tradition: *Seypevr Heyy'* (Life Stories,) where members took turns speaking of their histories and experiences.

Jethro Dag rose first from where he'd been occupying an entire blanket. He'd qualifying for the paratroopers at the maximum weight a silk canopy could carry and served under Colonel Rafael Eitan in the 1967 war. His nickname was 'Big 'Fish' ('*Dag* in Hebrew.) His unit was glad to have him. He could carry a German MG42 heavy machine-gun as if it were a plastic toy.

The Wanderers were in belly laughs when he described how his Dutch wife made his clothes when they were not so well off. "Ruth buys canvas. Holds it against me and says, 'This will look nice! Trust me!' Friends I have trusted her always, since she first laid her cheek against this piece of granite I call my face. *Ashety at hheyyem, shel!*" (My wife, my life!)

Rivka Beckman, a tall, attractive, 28-year-old redhead, described her life growing up in Kibbutz Neve Yam, where her grandparents had been founders of the Gordonia Zionist Youth Movement, and her husband Ari her childhood love.

Neve Yam occupied a piece of salt-marshy coastline just over an arched bridge from the British Occupation's Atlit Detention Camp. The guards had no clue that it was a base for the Palyam (Jewish Resistance Navy.) Or that those cheerful suntanned children in khaki shorts and shirts, passing them by, were smuggling supplies and messages under the rear wire.

Neve Yam's fish-processing plant was connected by a track to the beach where a rusty Massey-Fergusson tractor launched and retrieved the fishing boats. The children would flock like seagulls to see the precious cargos of tuna and bream.

A few listening nodded and smiled, remembering their own sunlit Kibbutzim summers. They knew how passionate Rivka still was about Neve Yam, where she was now treasurer. She surprised them by saying, "I'm giving that up. I've enrolled to learn literature at the University of Haifa, this fall."

Uzi Perlman, the handsome and outgoing company paymaster, got to his feet. The gathered knew he was a published poet, a hero of the 1973 war, and had gained his permanent limp fighting the Egyptian 3rd army at the Suez Canal. He congratulated Rivka and said he was also studying part time for English and German degrees at the Open University. He hoped she would get just as much *geshmack* (satisfaction) from her studies.

Stout, swarthy, Avner Geffen talked about how he still grieved for his parents. He'd been seven years old when they had been rounded up and shot in the street in Vsondovic, Poland, in random reprisal for a Molotov cocktail thrown at a Wehrmacht motorcycle dispatch rider. He'd come home to a cold house.

Last was Harel Abadi, a square-jawed, Moroccan-born Jew with dark features and kind almond eyes. There was a catch in his throat as he spoke of the Arab family who'd taken him in when he'd been orphaned. After 'Making Aliyah' to Eilat on the Red Sea through the Jewish Youth movement, his fluent Arabic had earned him a prime Egged Tour Guide's job.

But the pestering of bored young children had reached a crescendo. The day was cooling fast, and a shower looked imminent. Carry-bags were repacked, errant young people corralled, then they climbed the hill and re-boarded bus 88-191.

Gabriel Hahn drove down the hill on a reverse course to bypass Tel Aviv and see them safely home to Haifa via coastal Highway 2. He looked at his watch. 2:02 p.m.

Jerusalem

Shaul Weizman, the 31-year-old son of the present Defense Minister, was enjoying speeding down the hills of Judea in his beloved BMW 3.3LI. He was going to Netanya, the largest city on the south-central coast, but not looking forward to his meeting there.

The meeting was important, or it wouldn't be happening in the Shabbat. In fact, national security would be affected. But that was his job, political middleman, or hatchet-man, some would say. That was the case today.

Shaul's family connections gave him an almost unique perspective on Israel's problems. Most of them sprang from the special relationships between the country's political and military universes, going right back to the founder of the nation; David Ben Gurion, on whose knee he'd played as a child.

Politicians got too involved, too often, in tactical military matters. True, you couldn't get elected Kibbutz Toilet Cleaner without the military's support. Conversely, Generals and Admirals with even a whiff of charisma, routinely joined the Knesset after their uniformed careers. It wasn't like America where it was arms-length. Here, nepotism went hand-in glove. Bad decisions occurred regularly. That was happening again today.

Back in 1974, the Muslim DFLP out of Lebanon had raided Ma'alot, just over the border. A busload of children had been overnighting at a school. The Army's Sayeret Matkal, known as Two-Six-Nine in military parlance, bungled a rescue attempt. More than two dozen mostly young people died, proving that for all their finely tuned lethality, Israel's Elite Forces weren't suited to saving lives.

Shamed authorities had formed a new police unit called Yamam, modeled in the German post-Munich massacre, GSG-9. A just-retired 31-year-old Major of the paratroopers, named Mordechai 'Mordy' Zaks, was put in charge. Solemn promises were made that Yamam would the nation's primary domestic-hostage rescue force. He was an enormously physically gifted man who Weizman liked and admired. In his teens he could have topped the professional tennis circuit if he hadn't put his country first. Yamam, usually called the 'Unit,' were soon ranked with the best in the world.

But believing the military to give up their domestic defense role, purely on an edict, had been a pipe dream. The Sayeret Matkal, boosted by their rescue of the 256 hostages in the raid on Entebbe, had re-trained and reclaimed their lost space. Weizman was on his way to tell Mordy Zaks that Yamam was being relegated to an on-call unit for local events the regular police couldn't handle.

Weizman was obsessive about being on time for meetings. He'd promised to be in Netanya by 3:00 p.m., which seemed plenty of time, but still...

Better not keep the condemned man waiting.

He punched the accelerator and felt a satisfying push-back into the bucket-set, as the Beemer rocketed ahead.

Or Akiva

In a small town beside Highway 2, 49-year-old Galya Shumansky (Gali to her many friends,) and her 56-year-old husband, Yosef, were at their daughter

Maya's kitchen table. Yosef's sister Bracha was standing at the sink-bench making tea.

They were chatting in a mixture of Hebrew and Yiddish (Gali's preferred language,) about driving north to Haifa's Talpiot markets, which would open with the first stars of dusk.

More than that, they were relishing life, as only those who have survived the utmost in horror and privation, truly can. Yosef and Bracha were Dolghinov Jews, among the last survivors of a town in eastern Belarus, who had trekked to safety across hundreds of snowy miles of Russia Steppes in the deep winter of 1942.

Gali went to refresh her lipstick. When she returned to the lounge, no one was there. She heard car doors being opened in the driveway, so picked up her handbag and followed the noise.

The sky had cleared, and promised a lovely evening collecting *Kholov* cheese, *Banitsa* pastries, *Achva* cakes, and all the other treats. She was sure the *m'arm'l'ad* wouldn't be as good as hers. It was prized all over Ashdod.

Maya was driving. Gali joined Bracha in the back seat. *Ww'ás s dy yyaln?* (What's the sudden rush?)

Bracha made a "You know Yosef..." rueful grin.

Gali grinned too.

What a schlemiel! We have all the time in the world. The market won't open for ages!

It was 3:42.

HaTikva

In a South Tel Aviv suburb around that same time, 37-year-old Oskar Lerner whispered, "You look fine, my dear!" as he helped his wife Eliza Lerner-Bergman in through the sliding side door of a white Mercedes L206 taxi-van.

She truly did look radiant, with her cloud of hair beautifully curled, and her sundress decorated with orange, red, and yellow flowers. She should. That morning she'd paraded before her husband in every dress suitable for a child's birthday party, to have him pick just the right one.

The van that provided door-to-door service between Israel's two largest coastal cities already had seven passengers. The couple made themselves comfortable on the rear bench seat

This would be the first gathering of the Oscar and Eliza's tight-knit extended family, since the recent *Laveyah* (funeral) of Oskar's adored mother. On that day, clasping her sobbing husband as his mother's casket was being lowered beside that of her late husband, Eliza had whispered, "At least how beautiful. Couples going to rest together. Perhaps we will too one day!"

The van driver, Jivan Grigoryan, a young Armenian student in his mid-20s at the Open University of Israel, cheating on his student visa to pay his bills, looked at them expectantly.

"Daniel Gardens!' Oskar called out. "We will show you exactly where, when we get close."

Jivan smiled as he ticked them off his booking sheet. All drop-offs in the same central area. The best kind of trip. He accelerated away toward the northern thoroughfare out of the city; Mordechai Namir Avenue, named after a late and beloved Tel Aviv mayor, which merged seamlessly with Highway 2.

TWENTY

Highway 2

Baba'a studied the highway and their surroundings, like he had numerous battlefields. Traffic down the hill from their left, would arrive without much warning. The greater volume would be from the south, where the big city was. It would be slowed by a long incline.

A limestone bank lined their highway-side. The divider between the lanes was more gravel than grass. The far side dropped off into brushy, open land. Beyond that was Zichron Yaakov, a Hebrew town big enough to have its own off-ramp a couple of hundred yards up the hill.

Without knowing it, they'd tramped right past the Arab settlement of Jisr Al-Zarqa. They didn't know Kibbutz Ma'agan Michael even existed.

Baba'a got the still-woozy Wael up and gave him an AKM and backpack. He took the man's arm and with Hussain, Jalal, Ramz, and Rami, ran across the deserted lanes to firing positions facing south. Dalal and her team remained crouching in place, gazing uphill.

Dalal was thinking of the American woman.

How could she walk the fields of my homeland when I'm forbidden?

That, and the stress of exerting her authority, incensed her. But she wasn't going to let it deflect her.

Yáfa. Yáfa is our mission.

They'd been blockading the highway less than a minute when a low, deep sound grew in the air. The engine of a large vehicle droning up the incline. They soon heard out the rumble of tires on roadway. Then the faint sound of voices singing in a foreign language. A red and white bus. Closer. Closer.

Hussain's AKM made the characteristic thudding sound of Russian-designed weapons. The volley lashed the bus.

Aboard the Wanderers bus over the last 15 minutes, the physically-slight kids had been playing I-can-see-you-but-you-can't-see-me, using the secret world beneath the seats. They'd constructed forts from carry-bags and kept giggles to a minimum to avoid alerting the evil, spoilsport giants above.

The lead criminals were 10-year-old David Abadi, livewire Nina Horvath, 4, cherubic 9-year-old Benjamin 'Benny' Coen, and little mischief-maker Davie 'Junior' Forman, aged 7. But the ringleaders were captured and the uprising quelled anyway, in the name of safety. They banished the POWs to the rear-row to play with books. Or toys. Or anything.

Rivka Beckman had given Alon a quick diaper change while Ari held Raviv. Ari looked like Popeye holding Swee'Pea, with his massive shoulder muscles. He was smaller than when he was with the commandos doing 10 mile runs and 50 pull-ups a day, but stayed chiseled and maintained his washboard-stomach, as a semi-professional footballer for the Zichron Ya'akov Eagles. He adored his wife and children above all else, and was missing the most important game of the season, to be with them.

Rivka got another song going. A club signature tune, Dov Mankiewicz' ode to the kibbutzniks, '*Ha'adama Hageu'la*', (The Land Redeemed.)

From Mir Kiryat the scent drifts down
Eucalyptus scent on the Sharon breeze
From the Hula Valley across the Jordan stream
To the Kineret shore and on beyond
Wafts the stirring scent of the land redeemed.

From Tabor's crest my eyes drink in
The terraced loam, the fretted fields
The brave settlements arrayed, Ginegar

Geshur, Shemer, Nitzanim
The girded belt of the land redeemed.

I hear the Gvanim sung, watch the Hora danced
Raise my voice and whirl along
And in the morn, I'll Boker Tov! ...

In mid-stanza, little Nina made a break toward the front of the bus. Her mother was ignoring her, making voice noises with all the big people. It was unbearable! She was going to run until she got some attention.

Lavan snared her with one arm and lifted her on into her knee in the row right behind driver Gabriel Hahn. Pressed her face against the little girl's and made blubbering sounds. Nina shrieked with happiness. Much better. *Mommy loves me after all.*

Gabriel squinted ahead at an unusual sight.

What the hell are these people doing on the road? Some people have absolutely no sense of safety! Should be jailed!

The windshield exploded.

Hussain had forgotten his training and emptied an entire 30-round clip on full-automatic. Riddling the windshield and going through to destroy the rear glass as well.

Baba'a cursed under his breath. *How many times have I told them to hold low?*

Dalal fired several shots from the other side of the highway, then clicked to automatic and emptied her rifle. Everyone else was blocked.

The bus weaved but straightened out and coasted on. The terrorists stared after it, ears ringing and aware of the stink of gun smoke.

Then, to their delight, the bus slowed to a halt beside the center divider several hundred yards up the highway. People spilled out. Distant voices clamored.

Bullets ripped at Gabriel's clothing. Glass fragments tore at his face. But he was only hit twice, in the right arm and shoulder. Flesh wounds. They turned his white shirt crimson, but were painless so far. He blinked the glass dust from his eyes, made out the lane margins, and started to pull up.

Behind him, little Nina had been shot in the face and fallen forward into the aisle. Several rows behind, Tania Janowicz lolled in her aisle seat, her face also a red mask.

Passengers clutched at arms and shoulders and shed glass fragments from faces and hair. Amid the whirling of objects whipped up by an instant gale, few realized they'd been shot at. Hussain's gunfire had blended with the crash of the windshield caving in. Most believing they were in a traffic collision.

Reuvan stood gaping on the Highway 2 overbridge, his nicotine addiction forgotten. The gunfire had made him look down the highway to see a red and white, out-of-control juggernaut, hurtling at him. He grasped the bridge-railing with white knuckles. But the bus slowed to a halt yards before the center-piling.

When Gabriel relaxed his hands, the pain hit him like knife-stab. He collapsed groaning over the wheel. Judith rushed to his side. Someone else pushed the lever to open the doors, Passengers climbed out, baffled and asking each other, "*Eikh ho-Lekh?*" (What's happened?)

Reuvan gawked a moment longer at the frontal damage to the bus, then wheezed his way down from the overbridge.

At the shooting site, empty magazines clattered onto the road, and replacements were jammed home. But the bus was in the distance and hostages were already escaping. Then they heard engine noise and turned to find the solution to how they would get to the bus.

Jivan had been relishing the drive, with the Mercedes shuttle-van pulling strongly up the long slope. He was studying Hebrew. Eavesdropping on his passengers was a guilty pleasure, as well as good practice. The couple in the back were going to a 7-year-old's birthday party. The Jewish lady was showing her husband a swimsuit she'd brought as a gift. She was going to buy all the kids pizza.

Then he noticed men on the highway, and a lot more activity in the distance. One of the men was waving him down at gunpoint.

The terrorists wrenched open the van's side-door. The seven people who climbed out were holding their hands up and speaking Arabic. They were allowed to run away down the highway, along with the driver. Then Ramz ducked his head inside and saw a bewildered-looking man and woman in the very back. They didn't seem to comprehend anything shouted at them. Ramz kept his gun on the couple while hollering, "*Yalla! Yalla!*" (hurry) at his companions. The terrorists piled into the van with everything they had. Baba'a seized the wheel, and they roared up the highway after their prey.

Through all this, to drivers passing by, the terrorists hadn't looked like an armed band. They'd been focusing on the commotion farther ahead. Some cars went by obliviously. Several stopped, without any idea what they were getting into.

TWENTY-ONE

Taninim

Reuvan got to road-level and shouted, "Move over to the southbound side of the road. I will take you to my Kibbutz to get you help!"

Not all the shocked 40-or-so passengers who'd spilled off the Wanderer's bus heard him. Around eight remained milling in the center divider, and nine others sat comforting each other at the foot of the overbridge steps. Lavan stayed on her knees by the bus's open doors, howling in grief and hugging Nina's small blood-soaked body. Among the 22 who'd stayed aboard were Dubi Janowicz and his youngest boy, 10-year-old Ilan. The older one, Eitan, had been swept outside with the crush of people and was one of those near the scrub at the roadside. Dubi was kneeling in the aisle attending to Tania, who was lying between two rows of seats. Her skull was deformed by a bullet wound, but she was half-conscious and gasping for water.

Meanwhile, four cars had stopped nearby. The first two to arrive were from the north. Aboard one was Johann Tischner, a 29-year-old sales representative. In the other, a couple in their 20s named Elijah Kirschbaum and Monica Kreisel. Tischner was mixing with the passengers, seeing where he could help. The young couple were rummaging for a first aid kit.

The first of the two cars from the south, carried 60-year-old Nehemia Klein, a retired General Commissioner of Israeli Police, heading to a reunion in Haifa from his home near Beit Shemesh. In the second were the Dolghinov survivors, the Shumanskys, on their way night-shopping.

Baba'a had harangued the rest of the terrorists during the 45-second race north. "Let no one escape! No one!" He skidded to a halt near the bus's rear door, and the terrorists poured demonically out of the van.

They had rehearsed this scenario many times at Damour. Ramz pointed his AKM in the air and fired a short salvo, then leapt up the rear steps of the bus and fired more shots into the ceiling. Half the others ran around the off side of the bus. The rest charged across the road toward the passengers in the open.

Rami, in mid-stride, looked to his right and saw Gali, Yosef, Bracha, and Maya Shumansky. They wheeled and ran back toward their car. Rami fired from the hip, knocking Yosef and Gali down on the roadway. The rounds hit Bracha in her right shoulder, and Maya in the wrist, but they helped each other get behind their car and drop flat.

Ex-Police-Commissioner Klein was channel surfing on his CB radio to call for help, but seemed to be in a reception blind-spot. He watched the small terrorist open fire so coldly and accurately, then flopped onto the front bench seat. He steeled himself for a storm of bullets to come through the door-panel.

Elijah and Monica also ducked down in their front seats. They wriggled across and out passenger's door, then lay down with the car between them and danger, hardly daring to breathe.

By a miracle, like Klein, Rami overlooked them. For some unaccountable reason, he just turned and followed his companions out of sight.

These ear-shattering bursts of sound electrified those in the open. Everyone near the bus stared in dread at the guns trained on them, then lifted their hands or pulled children close. Those near the scrub scattered into it. Several terrorists tried to fire on them, but hadn't taken off the safeties from being in the van. Only Tariq got his gun working, causing several to stumble and one woman to fall just out of sight of the road. Children, including Eitan Janowicz, had no chance to say goodbye to parents and brothers and sisters, not knowing if they would ever see them again.

With the wild-haired terrorist leader shouting unintelligibly at them, the captured Wanderers shuffled together like corralled animals.

The terrorists had seized 49 people, including Good Samaritan Tischner, who right then was wondering what in hell he'd gotten mixed up in. The attackers whooped and catcalled, jabbing with their rifles at those who weren't hurrying enough. Grinning made Tariq look wolfish. And Fayadh, simply evil.

Gina 'Missy' Abadi, a 1-year-old in Marion's arms, roared. Little boys howled while their mothers tried to calm them. Lavan Horvath screamed at being forced to leave Nina lying on the road. Her husband, Jacob, and several other men looked broken. Others stared at their captors with hatred, but carefully, so as not to endanger their loved ones.

Except big Jethro. He clenched and unclenched his fists, eyes blazing at the humiliation of his friends. Then he glared at Jalal, and perhaps the big Arab remembered Ms. Heinrich-Mamatow's words. He forced Jethro out of the crowd. They locked eyes for another moment, then Jalal shot Jethro several times in his broad chest.

Screams and shouts broke out, but the terrorists quickly beaten down any rebellion.

Jalal spat on the body, then calmly rejoined the others.

Pre-cut lengths of nylon were pulled from backpacks and the captive men's hands were tied, leaving a tail. Then each was forced back aboard and lashed into the window seats, spaced out as human shields. The old, and the women and children, were packed in around them. Dubi was dragged away from Tania and pushed to the rear. The Lerners from the shuttle van were also jostled aboard. Then the terrorists took up firing positions, Rami and Hiza'a with grenade launchers. Some stayed in the aisle, swinging their AKMs back and forth.

Dalal and Tariq demanded to know who'd been driving. When they learned it was Gabriel, they press-ganged the nearest capable-looking candidate, Moshe Coen, over his wife Rina's pleading. Broken glass was kicked out of the window-frames, and Moshe was made to turn the bus to face Tel Aviv.

Baba'a was restless. There was no plan other than to head south where the American woman pointed and create havoc. But they'd been stationary far too long, though it had been less than seven minutes since the first shots. He was surprised there'd been no more traffic.

Then he heard an engine approaching. He walked to the rear exit and stepped down onto the highway. Looked north and aimed his Kalashnikov up the hill.

TWENTY-TWO

Highway 2 north of Ma'agan Michael

We'll be late arriving in Jerusalem, Sheena Ben Har mused to herself. *The boys have sports practices tomorrow and we haven't even reached Hadera yet. Enoch needs to get off his backside.*

Sheena wouldn't have said so, but the Ben Hars were no ordinary family, by Israel's standards or of any literature and music loving country.

Their Ford Fairlane 500 station-wagon was a large car for Israel, but habits linger. They were American immigrants who'd Hebraized their name to 'People of the Mountains' after their home state of Oregon. Enoch had been a prodigy at the Julliard and was now First Flutist with the Jerusalem Symphony Orchestra. Sheena was a renowned flutist as well, and daughter of Hebrew poet and novelist, Benyamin Stegelson.

But their weekend away at Amirim, in the Galilee hills, had been to honor the real star of the family. Seth, a small-built 14-year-old, sleeping with his brothers in the rear, was just home from a European tour as star clarinetist with the Jerusalem Youth Orchestra.

The station wagon cleared a crest and began descending past the sparkling fishponds of a roadside kibbutz. The Sharon Plain sprawled out before them. Sheena noticed heaps of glass glinting beside a bus facing away in the center divider. There were cars stopped at odd angles on both sides of the two-lane. Then she realized the red-splashed mounds ahead were bodies.

A bearded man in military dress got down. He pointed something north. Enoch had seen it too. Sheena rocked forward against her seatbelt as the brakes came on hard. The object in the man's hands twinkled. The shattering of their windshield and the hammer blows of bullets came as a single rolling sensation.

Enoch yelped, and his right hand dropped loose off the wheel. His arm spurted blood where a bullet had struck above the elbow, breaking the arm-bone and tearing-apart nerves. A terrible injury for a right-handed professional musician.

But Sheena breathed out in relief. She hadn't yet seen how seriously Enoch was hurt, and the gunfire seemed to have passed between them. One bullet had gone through her seat-back. Then she looked behind and screamed. Seth's face was a disfigured red mask.

Somehow, one-handedly, Enoch brought them to a stop in the middle of the southbound lane. He got out, holding his ruined arm against his stomach. Sheena scrambled into the back.

"No, no, no, no..."

She held her beloved son in her arms.

Ahead, a diesel engine revved as Egged bus 88-191 gathered speed along the highway.

Ma'agan Michael

Reuvan led his distressed group into the packing shed just before 4:45 pm.

Dubinsky stood up, outraged. The crowd of people were babbling. He heard "*taoonah*" (traffic accident,) mentioned and closed his mind completely.

"I don't want to hear about it," he shouted. "There's enough going on at the beach. I'm expecting visitors any minute. Now get these people out of here and do what you have to do!"

"But..."

"Now Reuvan!"

He shepherded the confused passengers outside. "Wait here!"

He ran as fast as his bulk allowed for his sister's unit.

Zichron Yaakov

Druze Police Constable Hamid Ba'asha was putting every ounce of his frayed patience into speaking politely on the phone. "Yes, I'm sorry the council people are closed on Shabbat, but I'm certain they'll come and fix your pothole soon Ma'am. But please call 106 the next time. Shalom!"

Hamid's curse was he hated soccer. So he always got stuck running the station on the big game days. And this was the biggest. Beach United versus the local Eagles. Almost the whole town was there. And every other officer on duty. To keep the peace, of course.

Mamzers! (Bastards) should have been back half an hour ago!

He could tell it was an exciting match. There'd been firecrackers, lots of them. But he had several calls logged on the sheet and needed someone to check out a problem with an Egged bus on the two.

The phone rang yet again. "Constable Ba'asha!"

"There's been shooting on the coastal highway!"

"Who's speaking, please?"

"Reuvan Erlich. I'm a security guard at Ma'agan Michael. There's..."

151

"We've already had calls. Some officers will be over there shortly."

"I am telling you it's terrorists!"

Hamid sighed. *Why me?*

"I'm sure you're mistaken, sir. Look, we'll be over there soon. Thank you."

Two officers sauntered in looking pleased.

"Fireworks keep you busy?" said Hamid. "Anyway, there's some bus problem on the two by the overbridge. Go have a look, would you please?"

As the two officers walked out to their car, one raised an eyebrow. "Fireworks?"

His partner grinned back. "I couldn't hear a thing for the cheering. What a great game!"

Within another minute there was a screech of tires and clattering of car doors. The front door crashed open. A middle-aged couple helped a woman inside. Her left side was scarlet. "Help us please! She's been shot! We found her beside the highway!"

Hamid dived for the radio hand-piece. Pressed 'send' and bellowed, "Zee-arr seventeen. Zee-arr seventeen. It's a terrorist attack. Acknowledge seventeen!"

In seconds he had the emergency-procedures and notification-numbers sheet out on the counter, a phone in each ear, and was taking turns talking tersely into each.

Highway 2 a quarter-mile south of Ma'agan Michael
Jeri Karam, driving Egged's express-bus 901 to Haifa, was being cautious. Two vehicles had flashed their lights in the last 30 seconds. A speed-trap, no doubt. *Ah well, the Meeshtarah (traffic cops) have their job to do even on Shabbat.*

Broken glass twinkling ahead drew his attention, and he touched the brakes. A fellow Egged bus in the new colors faced him in the center divider. Maybe it had hit the white van parked crookedly nearby. A male figure climbed down from the bus. The banana-shaped magazine of an AK-type weapon was unmistakable. The man pointed it away from him, and there was a billow of smoke.

Terrorists! I'm carrying passengers!

He was coming up on a stretch of packed gravel in the divider, there to let traffic turn left into Jisr Al-Zarqa. Jeri wallowed his bus in a half-circle and pounded the accelerator to the floor.

TWENTY-THREE

Southbound on Highway 2

The terrorists were crowing like cockerels aboard the Wanderers bus. They had 48 helpless and terrified people in their control and nothing to restrain them. Their happy grins became brutal leers.

Dubi had been catatonic when he'd been forced aboard. His hands weren't tied. He'd just been shoved into a rear aisle-seat. Now he needed desperately to reach Tania, who was moaning for water in a seat-well up front.

The first time he got up, Ramz shouldered him back into place. The second time, Dubi made it two steps up the aisle. Ramz shoved him flat and fired a flurry of shots into the Israeli's back, setting his cotton shirt smoldering.

Nearby hostages shrank away in horror. Mothers turned their children's faces into their breasts.

Ramz swung his right boot into Dubi's twitching body and smirked at Fayadh and Tariq. "*In lam yakun adore' ela alaql 'a token tahdhira* (If not a shield he can at least be a warning) he growled. The other two sniggered, and together they threw the blood-soaked body into an empty seat in back.

There were shouts from up front and the terrorist's moods swung mercurially yet again. There was another bus ahead. This one older and blue and white, and swerving, trying to get around traffic. "A bus! A bus! Don't let it escape!"

Baba'a rushed to Dalal's side at the driver's seat, where she had her rifle jammed into Moshe's neck. Baba'a yelled, "Yalla! Yalla!" When the driver was too slow responding, Baba'a mashed his foot down on top of Coen's.

Jeri was in a vice. The red and white bus behind him had sped up while traffic ahead was slowing. He swung the wheel hard left, praying not to tip over in the divider. Passengers screamed and shouted as they were jolted around. None had seen anything ahead before the U-turn. Now something was terribly wrong.

Dov reeled up from the back. The two Egged men spoke, then Dov pulled down a tour-guide's microphone. "We saw trouble and are avoiding it. Please hold on to your seats!" He tried to think of calming words and failed. "Thank you everybody. Hold on!"

But with the Scania behind them again, and traffic speeding toward him head on, Jeri had to steer back into the right lane. He watched in his rear-view mirror as the chasing bus nosed menacingly up almost against his rear. It swung outward and Jeri steered into them. A terrorist waved his rifle from a window. Jeri grimly ignored him. Then the Scania moved left onto the divider, and a bullet-storm thrashed Jeri's rear tires. The gunfire also climbed up the side of 901.

There were gasps and cries. Daniel the carpenter slumped dead. Moshe the salesman on holiday, doubled over with an exit wound in his belly. Glass and metal chips flew. Jeri's steering wheel juddered in time with the rubber flapping. He had to slow down. When both vehicles were at walking speed, three terrorists jumped between the two vehicles, fingers on triggers.

Jerusalem

Constable Ba'asha's first emergency-call had rung at the Police National Operations Center. Lieutenant Colonel Gavriel 'Gabe' HaAv hastened to the phone. The brisk and efficient man had a lot of experience with violence, having also been a Commander in the Haganah during the War of Independence.

"Terrorists at Ma'agan Michael?"

"On the highway near there, yes sir!" confirmed Hamid.

"What have you done so far? Sent a car? Good."

"Yes, but the bus is gone. There are just some abandoned vehicles, a Magen David Adom ambulance picking up bodies, and a lot of cartridge casings. Seven-point-six-two short."

"Not a surprise!"

"No sir. Our men have headed on to the kibbutz. A witness called us from there."

"Who else knows?"

"I'm talking to Sharon right now," Hamid said.

Police Headquarters, Central Plain

'Sharon' was the Regional HQ at Kfar Saba, just east of Highway 4 where it ran parallel with the two. Thirteen miles northwest of Tel Aviv. Sharon was responsible for the entire plain north to Haifa, except the beach city of Netanya. Two officers were in the squad room listening to Ba'asha's voice coming in on a desk-speaker.

Station Commander Elisha Neufeld, was a burly, no-nonsense, do-it-by-the book officer with gray hair at 37. Beside him was Inspector Levi 'Lev' Boker, a slim and blond, Australian-born 29-year-old. He was traffic commander and station second-in-command. His high rank for his age was because of a 'New

Policing' wave sweeping out the dinosaurs and breaking down old fiefdoms. Elisha had great confidence in his team of young up-and-coming officers and gave them a free hand.

Lev was having to concentrate to follow the thickly-Arab-accented Hamid. Then the constable said, "Hold one second," and broke away.

Back again, he said, "Our men have talked with some distraught passengers. The bus was full and they have family still aboard. They don't know which way it headed. Also, the senior man at Ma'agan Michael, a reserve Aluf, says his people found some rubber boats on the beach, and he's called out the Magav."

Oh shit! thought Lev. *Nothing quite like another agency crawling over your patch in a crisis.*

Elisha's reaction was similar. The border police liked to throw their weight around in the name of national security. *How the hell are we going to handle this?*

Highway 2 at Or Akiva

Jeri had opened the doors of 901 rather than provoke more shooting. He heard the attackers' boots on the rear step over the final bumping of the tires. Turned off the engine and kept his hands high on the wheel. Prayed they'd overlook his trying to run them off the road. Opposite him, Dov sat with his hands above his shoulders. Steeled for death, they waited out what might be the last moments of their, and their passengers', lives.

But the terrorists only ran up the steps and shouted. Jeri knew enough Arabic to know they were ordering everyone to exit. He stood up with hands high, called on his passengers to obey, and began leading them off the bus.

Tariq began kicking someone who'd been slow in getting up, as the victim cowered in their seat with arms protecting their face. He believed they'd captured a uniformed soldier. Instead, it was a 17-year-old boy named Karl Radek, who'd let his Aunt talk him into having a photo taken in his beige and epauletted shirt from Haifa's Technion School, before catching his ride home. Leaving it on was the worst decision of his life.

Dov watched the beating with icy anger, but there was nothing he could do. There were gun-muzzles in his face. He could only go along quietly with everyone else and pray for his opportunity to come. But there was even less chance of escape outside. An 8-foot stone-block wall lined the highway to protect the wealthy residents of Caesarea from traffic noise. Escapees would have to run exposed either up or down the highway. Guaranteed death waited in both directions.

Fayadh strutted around at the foot of the bus's front steps like a gamecock. When Sapira Lindner tried to ease her arthritic hips down to the ground, he swung at her with his rifle butt to hurry her along. The bus driver, all five feet four of him, rushed out of the crowd, and breasted him.

"Don't!"

One of these is challenging me? These thieving Zionists?

He leveled his weapon but would have to fire into the backs of valuable hostages, which wouldn't be popular.

Wael arrived and prodded the driver away, allowing the older people to climb down.

The driver went along.

TWENTY-FOUR

Sharon Police HQ

Alisha and Lev were in the Sharon operations room, on separate phones, struggling to coordinate a response with the other west-side stations.

Elisha said scathingly as he hung up, "Haifa station is waiting for direct orders from on high. *Yahweh* (God) maybe."

Lev shrugged. "Well, that's Karel."

Karel Kohler, the man in charge up there, was being sidelined pending retirement. He was a famous ditherer.

"And the constable at Zichron Yaacov says the Magav have roped his men into their search along the coast," added Elisha.

Nothing was forthcoming from Hadera or Caesarea either. Netanya, though not in their district, had promised support if Sharon could give them a specific mission.

Elisha asked, "Can Jerusalem do anything more?"

"Gabe HaAv is notifying Commissioner Tavori. No word back yet."

"Well, looks like it's down to us for now."

"Yes sir."

Lev wished the other two senior Sharon men were there. Inspector's, Joshua 'Josh' Leider, the Operations Officer, and Hani Urman, who ran the Uniformed Division. They were out on calls in the Hadera area, though in touch by radio.

Elisha traced his finger over the incident site on a wall map. "At least there's consensus they went north. No-one lands in north Israel to attack the south. Either the Magav will find them or we'll get a sighting and can zero in on it."

"They're wrong," Lev said. "Fatah will be behind this and they'll want to make the biggest impact. That's Tel Aviv. I promise you they're headed south!"

He tapped beside the blue grid of the Ma'agan Michael fishponds a few times. "Just suppose. It will have taken them a while to control the hostages, perhaps ten minutes." He glanced down at his wristwatch. "Four-fifty-two now, so they might have made it to about... here."

Lev circled two intersections on Highway 2 at Olga. Fourteen miles south of the original event. A major crossing at Yishai Street, and a smaller one a hundred yards south again, at HaShalom Street.

"We need to get Josh and Hani, to here and here, before the Arabs, and set up a main and a backup block."

"That's if these animals are headed that way," said Elisha.

"I'll stake my life on it. Tel Aviv's the target!"

"You are betting more than just your own. Can they make it in time?"

"It's a ten-minute run for them, give or take. All they need is to hold them there. We'll get them some backup, somehow."

"And if they don't get there in time, or can't stop them. What then?"

"We'll keep trying until we do. Allowing these monsters anywhere near Tel-Aviv on a Shabbat night doesn't bear thinking about!"

"And you, Lev?"

"I've got a backup plan. But let's see if Josh and Hani can find and stop them first."

"Okay. Keep me informed, please."

Or Akiva

There was sudden gunfire from the road-facing side of the two stopped buses. Rami had seen two vehicles coming from the south. The car in front kept going at a normal speed as if the driver hadn't noticed. The van behind swerved, then drove off the edge of the highway and rolled from sight.

The action galvanized the terrorists' efforts to get all their hostages onto the one bus. Some were cowering and crying. Others held on to their dignity while the Arabs split the men off from the rest.

Joe Hallwany protested. A big terrorist swung his rifle butt against the elderly man's back. Jeri breasted him. "They are in my care. Mine. Don't touch!"

The gunman didn't seem to understand a word, but drew back anyway, perhaps in respect at the angry little Israeli's courage.

Reenacting their work at Taninim, the terrorists tied all the men's hands. Even the harmless elderly. They trussed Jeri into the last-seat-but-one on the right side. Then everyone else was crammed aboard the Scania. Making 88 people jam-packed into a bus built for 52.

Dalal had taken off her flag, leaned over the driver and tied it to the bus's wing mirror as a streamer. Rami, Hiza'a, and Jalal, loaded rocket launchers and took positions at the rear side windows, forcing those around them even tighter into rows away from the weapons' back-blast.

At 4:51 p.m. Dalal jabbed the driver in the back twice, then made furious gestures no one could have misunderstood. He pulled out onto the highway, leaving 901 and a scattering of shiny cartridge cases where they'd been.

Tariq and Hussain at the windows began sniping at traffic. Several rocket grenades flew from the rear windows with far more visual than destructive effect. The explosions forced more vehicles to veer off the highway. The occupants joined others already escaping on foot.

One car had stayed occupied. A small white Renault. Fifty-three-year-old Shalev Koffman, in the driver's seat, was by pure coincidence the Egged manager of many of the captured Wanderers. He'd been driving south with his wife Carmela for a family visit to Ramat Gan, Northeast Tel Aviv, when he'd realized there were two Egged buses behind him, one shooting at the other. He'd pulled up ahead.

Shalev had been a warrior most of his life. First with the British in WWII, and then as a founder of the IDFs Carmeli Brigade, Battalion 21, with whom he'd fought in most major battles of the Independence War. It wasn't in his nature to run away from danger.

He'd been watching from what felt like a safe distance, over the rim of the rear windshield. Trying to get the best information for any authority he could then find. Suddenly the newer of the two buses pulled out, and Shalev realized he and Carmela weren't safe at all. His arms prickled with adrenaline.

He grabbed the ignition key, but the car wouldn't start. That had been an off-and-on problem over the past week. He had the car booked in for service after the weekend. The bus was now only two hundred yards away. He thought of ducking down in the seat beside Carmela. But what if they'd already been seen? He kept cranking.

The engine caught. Shalev had his foot crookedly on the clutch pedal. It slipped off. The car bunny-hopped and stalled.

No point in trying to hide now.

He frantically started it again, jammed it in first gear and planted the accelerator pedal.

Baba'a and Dalal both called out, "Car. Shoot! Shoot!"

Rami leaned out a side window and fired off-hand at the moving Renault. The first rounds only kicking up macadam chips. His second attempt riddled the car, killing Shalev and wounding Carmela. The Renault veered left, bounced off a stationary car, and stopped clear of the southbound lane.

The terrorists exulted as if their team had scored a winning touchdown at the Superbowl.

Wael broke into a song, the Palestinian revolutionary anthem, 'Mawtini - My Homeland.' He stumbled over the first few words, but relaxed into the better-known second verse. Others joined in. They sounded like a tone-deaf Russian men's chorus singing backward.

My homeland, my homeland,
The youth will not tire
Their goal is your independence
Or they die, or they die.
We will drink from death,
and will not be to our enemies
Like slaves, like slaves.
We do not want, we do not want
An eternal humiliation, nor a miserable life.
We do not want, but we will bring back
Our storied glory, our storied glory.
My homeland, my homeland.

Bus 88-191 raced on south toward crowded and unsuspecting Tel Aviv.

TWENTY-FIVE

East of Olga

Inspector Hani Urman's knuckles were white on the wheel of his black and white Ford Cortina police car, as it raced along an unsealed road parallel to the Coastal Road, the final few hundred yards to the southern of the two Olga crossings.

He and Josh Lieder had exchanged a few crackly words via the overloaded car-radio network He knew his friend was heading just as fast for the busier northern crossing.

Now it was at 4:56 p.m. It'd be anybody's guess whether they'd be in time to close Highway 2 before the terrorists passed, but it wouldn't be for lack of trying. He kept on pushing the accelerator pedal through the floor.

Josh had made better time and was rounding the last bend on Aharon Aaronson Street with the Yishai crossing straight ahead. An Hadera police car had its nose up to the intersection. His hopes lifted. Someone had answered his calls for support from any officer in the vicinity, and he wouldn't be alone in this. The traffic-lights were rhythmically flashing orange, and the uniformed officer was out of his car wearing his white gloves. Josh drove around the officer and placed his car in the middle of the empty intersection, then got out to make a plan. He'd taken two steps when the Hadera officer stopped waving his arms and stared north.

With a strange sound, part wind-whistle, part engine-roar, a passenger bus missing its windshield and trailing a Palestinian flag from the driver's wing-mirror, plunged toward him at terrifying speed. What might be rocket launchers jutted from side-windows.

In the name of... God!

Josh's mind flashed they would find him dead with his .38 revolver still holstered.

The bus swerved to avoid his police car, adding protesting tires to the cacophony. Gun muzzles protruded and blazed from the left side windows, the bullets tearing away overhead.

Josh dived flat, aware the other officer was doing the same. When he lifted his head, the terrorists were receding. They were cheering.

Hani heard shooting even before he stopped at the HaShalom intersection. By the time he was out of the car with his revolver in his hand, the bus was already too close, so he ran around the back of his car and ducked down. He glimpsed faces staring from windows as it sped past. Some full of horror, others surrounded by unkempt hair and beards and contorted with anger. He got the impression the vehicle was packed, though most windows had curtains puled. He lifted his hand-gun impotently before lowering it again. His heart was a pounding boom-box within his chest.

One minute later, after a terse conversation with Sharon Station, Hani put his car-radio hand-piece back in the car as Josh drove up.

Josh's face was stark white.

"What?" Hani asked.

"I thought I was a dead man!"

"I imagine," said Hani, managing a grim smile. "Anyway, base says we follow. Not too close. Report in when we can. The radio coverage should improve."

"Let's go."

They waved to the Hadera police officer to fall in train, and the three vehicles headed south in fast pursuit.

Sharon Station

Lev and Elisha weren't by themselves anymore. Seven off-duty constables had arrived from homes near the station and were kitting up with riot gear. At least they had troops, if they could decide how to use them.

Lev let loose a string of swear words from his Australian upbringing, as he hung up from giving Hani and Josh their instructions. He ended with, "What a shemozzle!"

"Worse than that," said Elisha "Now they've got momentum. If they get as far as Tel Aviv, on a Saturday night, people out driving. Shoppers. People walking with their kids..."

"I know that Boss, so where's the next best place?"

"Nothing really, until near Netanya."

"I'm not so sure." Lev walked to the map. "I think there's a place around Beit Yanai." He pointed to the lake of that name, south of the coastal power station, then looked at his watch. 5:01 p.m. "Question is, can we get there with enough time?"

"How about from Netanya?"

Both knew Netanya Station was in turmoil, with a new leader and many new transfers.

"Let's bring them in, but not to the north. Say to provide a backstop... say around here!"

Lev was tapping on the major southern crossing south of Netanya in Kfar Shmaryahu, the northernmost suburb of Herzliya. Gunfire westward would be over open country around the Crusader-era ruins of Apollonia. Not totally safe for civilians, but saf-er. The problem was, Herzliya was only 10 miles north of Tel Aviv. But that was perilously close to Tel Aviv.

"And you?"

Lev, as traffic-head, knew the highway backwards. "I'll take four men to where it doglegs here at Havatzelet HaSharon. There's a line of trees that hides what's around the bend until you are right there."

"Okay." Elisha had little confidence, but even if he'd been a micro-manager, this was not the time. He had to trust his men.

"You'll need to handle comms if you will."

"Right."

"We need to get out an all-points bulletin right away. Jerusalem Ops can do that. Tell them we need any armed personnel, army, navy, air force, policemen. People on leave. Anyone with a weapon and the training. Send them here so we can squad them up, or......" He checked the map again. "To where Mordechai Namir merges with the two at Yunitsman Street."

That's right where Tel Aviv begins! "Right."

"Please tell Netanya they are looking for a red and white bus with window curtains, and if we don't stop these beasts we'll have a bloodbath."

This was the take charge attitude Elisha so prized in his officers. "I'm on it," he said.

Highway 2

Stress had been too much for many. 88-191 stank of urine and worse body matter, mingled with fear and burnt cordite. At least the wind-tunnel effect flushed the worst of it into their wake. The police were still following, but at a respectful distance. The terrorists had gone silent after their victory song, as they hurtled on southbound, swaying treacherously at even the least curve, though only for a minute.

There'd been an astonishing change. Most of the terrorists were smiling and slapping each other's backs, flush with hubris and imaginary omnipotence. Khaled and Hussain offered around cigarettes from blue packs of Gauloises Caporal. The hostages remained impassive, but several older people accepted, rather than trigger more violence. The nuggety little bus driver had one put in his mouth. He spat it out and crushed it under his shoe as soon as Hussain turned his back.

But Dalal was somber and restless. She left Moshe in Khaled's hands and navigated the slalom of spilt blood and cartridge cases down the aisle. She brushed past Wael, Ramz, Hussain and Fayadh, with their AKMs slung, to where Rami, Jalal and Hiza'a guarded the back. Then found she'd nothing to say to anyone.

Turning to go back, she glimpsed, down low, a small face with wide eyes, framed with blond hair. The child was all the way under the back seats.

A scene of peaceful Dbaiyeh flashed in her mind. She'd been fresh from her nursing training. The camp children had played by her side each day. Her relationship with Jihad was adding to her life instead of taking everything from it. She felt in her jacket pocket for a Nestlé candy bar she'd been saving since they'd been at sea and offered it. The child took it in her small hand.

Dalal rose guiltily, but all others were looking outside at momentary possible threat. She went back to her station behind the driver and touched him with her gun-muzzle to remind him not to do anything adventurous.

Tariq had found the overhead tour-guides' microphone and realized he had a true captive audience. He played with it until the overhead speakers hissed. "We are here to fight for our beloved homeland, but also for oppressed people everywhere. You Zionists cannot keep us from our lands forever. We will fight you and we will win!"

He name-dropped every warrior-philosopher's name he could remember, as if the captives could understand his rapid-fire Arabic even if they could hear it above the wind. Reality had never been his forte.

A state of surreal calm had come over many of the hostages.

Rivka, holding her own two young boys close, had her right arm back through the gap between her seat and the wall. She was holding onto and comforting, Ilan sitting behind her. Across the aisle, on her back between seat-rows, his mother's eyes were open and staring. The Janowiczs and Beckmans were best friends. The grief of their orphaned son was almost worse than their loss. She whispered, "Please be strong. We will get through this!"

Uzi's wife Sara was separated by several rows and the aisle, from her beloved warrior-poet husband. At least their children, Aria, 14, and Elon two years younger, were with him in the row behind. Their hands were holding his, still tied behind him. *Oh, my love, my love.*

In a window seat right behind the back doors, Dov seethed with anger. But he kept his face expressionless and body language subdued, as he worked on the knots behind his back. He was pretty sure he could pull loose if he tried. *Maybe then will come a chance. Just a chance!*

There was a commotion behind Dov. Followed a few seconds later by two solid crumping explosions.

TWENTY-SIX

Netanya

At an upscale condominium on Netanya's Yehuda Ha-Nasi Street, just 200 yards from a brilliant snow-white Mediterranean beach, a massive-shouldered, bull-necked man with a close-cropped dome of a skull and a jutting jaw, fought to keep the anger out of his voice, "So that's it?"

Shaul Weizman feigned cheerfulness. "Yes, afraid so. Status quo for now,"

"Status quo?" Mordy Zaks bit off the rest of a bitter reply.

There's no point in getting angry or having a shouting match. It's just hard being reasonable with these fuckers.

But it wasn't this young man's fault. Or his father's. Mordy had a soft spot for both war heroes. Ezer had won his Medal of Valor in the skies. Shaul on the front lines in Egypt. He'd have to face it,

Yamam's downgrading to a glorified swat team was just the collateral damage of budget cuts. And the army had more clout.

What hurts is I lost because I trusted those bastards. And it's my men who'll suffer.

Mordy rarely lost.

Bnei Brak

Inside another condo, in East Tel Aviv, a slim, sinewy-looking Police Inspector named Shimon 'Zeke' Ezekiel, sat in a Barcalounger with his nose in a voluminous paperback. The Leon Uris' novel 'Trinity' about the Irish troubles, had just become available in Israel. It wasn't 'Exodus' but Zeke was a history buff and he was finding it fascinating reading.

There were two radios on in the room. A regular transistor broadcasting pop music from Kol-Israel, and a police-band scanner blurting out occasional, mostly garbled, transmissions. The first because music soothed the soul. The second because Zeke was hoping something might pop up on it to solve a work crisis.

In early 1976 after completing his IDF service as a Lieutenant of the *Egoz* (IDF counter-guerrilla forces,) someone mentioned a new police unit called Yamam, a centrally based, first-call response unit for internal security events. It sounded a platinum opportunity.

A fitness fanatic who never missed a 2-hour morning workout, Zeke had flown through his *Gibush* (tryout) at the Wingate Center near Netanya, and had eaten up every challenge thrown at him. After being accepted, he'd risen fast to his present position of Yamam second-in-command.

But despite his fierce loyalty to his boss, lately his physical workout had become the high point of his day. No real missions were coming Yamam's way. They weren't even training with the IDF Special Forces any more. It chafed so much he was thinking of quitting. But you had to have hope, so Zeke, a caffeine addict, had his coffee machine bubbling in the kitchen and the radios going. He felt guilty at wishing for evil to respond to, but who knew what the day might bring?

A low, excited voice spoke over the scanner. Something unusual was happening with traffic north of Hadera.

But there had to be a national emergency, or a request for help from a regular police unit, before his unit could get called out. Still... He laughed at his eagerness. *Don't be crazy! What are the chances?*

He went back to the folks of Ballyutogue, Donegal, who were keeping the fairies at bay while laying old Kilty Larkin beneath the sod. *Tribal rituals. So many parallels with here.*

The emergency tones interrupted. He dropped his feet to the floor and listened. A voice spoke in precise Hebrew. Zeke came right out of his chair. It was an All-Points Broadcast. There was a threat moving south on Highway 2 from Ma'agan Michael, which he knew wasn't far south of Haifa.

Zeke grabbed the phone and dialed a well-memorized number. While it rang, he carried the phone over to a cupboard and one-handedly started dragging out his combat equipment.

Netanya

Mordy argued anyway. His men deserved at least that.

"Look they promised me," he said, hating himself for sounding plaintive. "They came to me! Said we'd be first up. Not second after the damn Two-Six-Nine. First!"

"Times change," Shaul said, shrugging.

"Be damned they do! They said they needed one force to handle terrorist situations inside the borders. I built that force, and it's the best on the planet!"

Weizman didn't doubt it.

"Not the point, Mordy. Most of our politicians were soldiers. You think they forget who put them there? And who can destroy them? My friend you've been outvoted!"

Mordy'd had such expectations for this meeting. Two weeks ago, he'd given the senior Weizman the full treatment at their base near Beit Shemesh.

inspections, demonstrations, the whole deal. His men had excelled. He'd asked Ezer what it took to get Yamam declared the go-to force. This was the bitterest of answers. Publicity had created Yamam. Only the same thing could cement home their value. Otherwise, they'd wither, get caught in a real budget crush and disband, with his skilled officers sent back to the beat.

He felt instantly ashamed.

How can I even think of a violent assault on my beloved country as anything but pure evil?

The phone rang. Mordy needed to finish this meeting as graciously as possible and go beat a tube of tennis balls to death, so he ignored it. His wife Deborah appeared from the kitchen, holding the hand-piece against her. She mouthed, "Zeke, Urgent."

A half minute later Mordy was watching the belt pager he never took off except for meetings, spit out a flood of codes. He roared with frustration. Into the phone he said, "I'm going north. Round up anyone else you can find and get yourselves ready. Anything changes radio me in my car on the 800 band."

Inside three more minutes, Mordy was running for the underneath parking. He was in dark-blue combat fatigues and a Kevlar vest with 'Yamam' across the front and back. In one hand was a 223 caliber, carbine version of the Galil assault rifle. From the other hung a holstered Sig-Sauer 9mm pistol attached to a web-belt of magazine-pouches.

He put the web-belt in the back and leaned the rifle against the passenger's seatback of his personal toy-car, a road-spec Datsun 1600 SSS rally-car. Then snarled up out of the basement and headed parallel to Highway 2 for the access ramp just north of Havatzelet HaSharon.

Netanya

Close by, on Reuven Barkat Street just off Netanya's main east-west thoroughfare, five policemen working under the Sharon Station commander's orders, were doing last minute checks.

They included Druze Sergeant Major Amin Bin-Amr, perhaps the most experienced in south Israel. Also, a sergeant and two bright and willing junior constables. But due to staff turnover, they were new to each other.

The leader, Inspector Jacob Haberman, felt intimidated by the senior enlisted man. A more assertive officer would have listened when Alisha Neufeld briefed them by phone. Instead, he'd delegated to Bin-Amr and gone looking for proper boots.

Just the same, they soon turned south onto Highway 2 at its busiest on-ramp, in two cars with Haberman and Bin-Amr riding together.

Bin-Amr pointed at a vehicle ahead. "That must be it!"

"What? Where?"

"The red and white bus!"

"How do you know?"

"They said it has curtains."

A large modern tour bus crawled along amid a small flock of slow traffic.

Haberman was astounded they had found the bus so easily. Promotion beckoned.

"Right! Let's get in front of it!"

TWENTY-SEVEN

Highway 2 south of Hadera

Josh and Hani had been doggedly trailing the Wanderers bus, at 50 MPH and a safe-ish distance of 150 yards, for over 10 minutes since the failed ambush at Olga. Other police cars had joined up, but all but one had peeled off to stop traffic joining the two at various on-ramps. Most recently, at Beit Yanai's 5720 junction. Traffic had dwindled to a trickle. But they'd still seen twenty or more vehicles shot up and shot at, but with no serious injuries.

They were on the last long stretch before the urban clutter around Netanya, with Josh leading, when two objects trailing smoke flew from the cavernous rear window and bounced toward them. Josh planted his brakes and threw his Ford into a sideways skid. He how thin-metaled little English sedan was and hoped to put its width between him and the explosives. Hani only saw Josh go sideways in front of him. His right front fender speared Josh's car behind the center pillar. Both vehicles skidded along, locked together.

One grenade felled a telephone pole, worsening a communications crisis by cutting off many phones north of Netanya. The other exploded in Josh's front-right-wheel-well, with an orange flash. That wheel flew off, and the crumpled front dug into the road, stopping both police cars within a few more yards.

Hani thanked his stars he'd been wearing his seat belt, flicked the release catch and leapt out. Josh was doubled forward, holding his left arm against himself, but wasn't bleeding.

"Are you okay?"

"Not sure. Broken forearm. Sore back."

"Let's have you out of there."

The driver's door was inoperable so Hani ran around to the passenger side. The car's front-right looked like it had been kicked by a giant's boot. They'd been lucky.

In another minute they were in the third police car, having left the officer to oversee the scene, and heading for the nearest hospital.

Havatzelet HaSharon

Barely four miles south of Hani and Josh's near miss, Lev and four other policemen were standing beside Highway 2. They hadn't noticed Mordy Zaks speeding by on the parallel road. Their black-and-whites were scattered across the lanes. They meant to position those strategically once they had the highway interdicted with road spikes.

What had attracted Lev here was a single line of Australian blue-gums in spring leaf, stretching away at a right-angle. The trees that old-hand kibbutzniks' said 'made Israel,' with their ability to find water where there was none while drying out the marshiest swampland. Perfect concealment from vehicles coming along the straight that began just around the curve.

Now Lev wasn't so sure. It worked both ways. They couldn't see what was coming either.

They started unloading long strips of the four-pointed metal devices that always landed with a two-inch spike pointing upright, but stopped still, when they heard two thudding explosions followed by the faint mangling of metal, to their north.

Options flashed through Lev's mind. He'd expected more time to set the trap. Now at a guess he had one, maybe two minutes. Not enough time to lay the spikes, get the cars parked, and find safe firing positions. And if the terrorists escaped the bus, the trees offered them great fire cover. Better to fight another time and in a place with greater advantages.

He hollered at the others to drop what they were doing and run to the coastal side of the highway where there was a two-foot drop. They just had time to draw pistols, before with a strange rushing of air and roar of its overstressed engine, the terrorist's bus careered into view.

Moshe saw the police cars and took his foot off the gas pedal. The woman terrorist shouted and jabbed his arm. That didn't stop him from hitting the brakes hard. If he steered around the police cars at the speed he was going, he'd roll. The mass of metal beneath him juddered down to a controllable speed.

Fifty yards out, Khaled said, "The cars are empty! The yellow-bellied Jews have run away!" Exuberant shouts echoed him. Then Tariq saw a policeman peer over the road edge and fired, knocking chunks off the road edge. Jalal emptied his magazine too, also hitting nothing.

"Go through! Go through!" screamed Dalal, jabbing Moshe again.

Lev's men thought the bus would go over the drop-off and roll on to them. They hugged the ground. But the bus's fender struck one police car and shoved it into another like flotsam. The Scania rocked on its suspension, but pulled back onto the tarmac under lumbering acceleration. The terrorists lobbed two more grenades as they sped away. They exploded with a flat spanging sounds on the road surface, but did no harm. As the tortured sound of the battered Scania receded, Lev hauled one of his men up by the collar and led them in a lumbering dash to the remaining cars.

Hadera

Josh and Hani's nearest hospital to the explosion-site was Hillel Yaffe Medical Center, about halfway back to where they'd started the chase. Famous until recently as a center for organ transplants, it was a fine accident and emergency hospital. Tragic footnotes to the destruction so far, were playing out at its emergency entrance.

Maya and her aunt Bracha, draped in bloody police blankets, were being helped down from a white ambulance. When they'd disappeared indoors, Gali and Yosef were lifted out a second vehicle and wheeled respectfully toward the morgue. The policeman who'd accompanied the ambulances had the police-emergency telephone cabinet open by the front entrance. He cursed because the system was overloaded and kicked the wall. Communications of all kinds were at a crawl nationwide. In the background were the faint but rising sirens of ambulances bringing other injured and worse from far and wide.

Hani helped Josh inside, expecting a very long wait.

Haifa

At the A&E entrance of Rambam Hospital on Haifa's waterfront, two private vehicles slewed to a halt at ragged angles to the forecourt. The occupants jumped out, screaming for help.

Out of the first, a woman lifted little mischievous Nina. A passing ex-IDF medic and his wife had thought she still had a chance. A doctor found a pulse and rushed her into the theater, but she lost her fight on the table.

In the other vehicle were the Ben Hars. Orderlies helped Sheena out of the back seat, the side of her dress crimson from holding Seth against her. Enoch was taken directly to surgery. A doctor checked Seth, but could only look tragically at Sheena. A nurse reached out in comfort, but couldn't prevent her from collapsing in the driveway. She cried inconsolably, as she was gathered in the loving arms of two of her remaining children, and helped to the hospital *Shul* (sanctuary).

Northbound out of Netanya

With his little pocket-rocket racing along the first good straight, and him steering with his knees,

Mordy Zaks reached for the in-car radio and hailed Zeke, who answered immediately.

"Mordy it's bad. I don't know what you've heard."

"A bus and terrorists."

"Two buses, but only one on the loose. Kohler from Haifa was just aboard the abandoned one. One dead. Another with a through-and-through stomach wound. Probably only alive because he's a big guy. Belly fat helps."

"Yes, lucky."

"The wounded guy estimated a dozen terrorists."

"Yehoshua!"

"Really. Where are you?"

"Near Havatzelet HaSharon, heading north. Uhhhhhhh wait one!"

Mordy had arrived suddenly at the 5720 junction four miles northwest of Netanya. He rounded the last corner and had to brake hard. A traffic officer was in the road, holding up a white-gloved palm. He had his other hand on his .38, having not yet noticed that Mordy was in full combat gear with 'Yamam' across his tactical vest. Mordy slapped his warrant card with its distinctive blue Star of David, against the windshield with his left hand, and said, "Are you there Zeke?"

"Yeah, well, you need to turn around. The loose bus is almost at Netanya."

"Shit! I must have just missed it!"

"Sharon desk sergeant says they still have a couple moves they can make south of there, I think at Kfar Shmaryahu and then Glilot, but it's a running battle. They've gotten through everything that's been put up so far."

"Dammit!" cursed Mordy. "Any word if they're bringing our men from Beit Shemesh?"

"I know the request has gone to the top of the Army, but I don't think it matters now. They'd never make it in time, even by heavy chopper. No Two-Six-Nine either. Same problem."

"All right, I'm heading south."

Mordy cinched the center buckle of the four-point safety harness as tight as he could.

TWENTY-EIGHT

Highway 2 south, north of Netanya

The clash with Lev and his men at the tree-obscured bend sent the terrorists into a black mood. Their thoughts had been darkening anyway, as the countryside became more urban. Townships were passing by with greater frequency. Netanya's high-rises were rising in the near distance.

The skirmishes with the police would become more frequent. There was no plan except to reach Tel Aviv and see what they could win from an inevitably one-sided battle.

In contrast, the 64 adult hostages seemed hypnotized into glum acceptance. The faces of their 24 children expressed uncomprehending fear. To anyone who didn't know the Sabra spirit, they would have appeared be a cargo in transit, cowed into submission, hoping their barter-value saved their lives. This fueled the evil in the terrorist' souls.

Jalal, Ramz and Fayadh struck out at every opportunity. Legs out too far because grown-ups overflowed a pair of seats, were kicked out of the way. An infant crying out for water or the toilet, saw the child and mother abused. Any variance from total submission drew cruelty. Then Fayadh passed by the Karl Radek. The boy was in tears.

He tormented the boy like a bully in a school playground. Bashing him with his gun-butt where his brow bled from an earlier assault and attacking his chest when the lad covered up. Other terrorists chortled. After several rounds Fayadh remembered his AK47 had a spike bayonet. He pricked the slight 17-year-old in the upper shoulder. Karl shrieked. Fayadh guffawed and looked around so the others could enjoy the moment.

Dalal watched the road ahead overly intently. Baba'a stared out the side window. Some others shifted uncomfortably. Tariq's eyes gleamed.

Fayadh jabbed again, harder. The bayonet-point deflected off the big arm bone and punctured an artery. Blood gushed. Karl screamed and fell into the aisle. The terrorist fiend stabbed and ripped at the fallen boy in a blood-lusting frenzy. His finger slipped into the trigger guard. The rifle fired, killing the boy and jerking the bayonet out of the body with the recoil.

Avner Geffen lost control. Despite his wife Leah's strong grip around his upper body, he screamed and kept on screaming.

Rami poked the muzzle of his gun in the man's face. But Avner had dissolved. Rami reversed the AKM and gave Avner a swinging blow that also battered Leah. Avner's screams were piercing and constant. Rami held his AKM on its side like a Crips gangsta holds a .45. Bullets ripped Avner's chest apart, also grazing Uzi's one good leg in the row behind. Leah's screams replaced her husband's until smothered in the arms of friends.

There came an unusual noise; a woman's voice, low and shaky at first, but growing in confidence. Rivka had spoken the first line of the '*HaTikva*,' the 'Hope,' the Israeli national anthem, which the Wanderers had sung countless times. Like a statement, 'As long as in the heart within.'

She turned as far as Raviv on her lap allowed, made an up-up motion with her hands, and said the phrase again. Rina Coen joined in halfway through, followed by Sara Perlman, then one or two husky men's voices.

The next line, 'A Jewish soul still yearns,' was full-throated. The following phrase, 'And onward, toward the ends of the east, an eye still looks toward Zion,' was strong even over the wind. Everyone Israeli punched the chorus hard.

Our hope is not yet lost,
The ancient hope.
To return to the land of our fathers,
The city where David encamped.

The terrorists stared, then their faces hardened.

Ramz, nearest to Rivka, snarled and reversed his AKM. Rivka pushed Raviv off her and stood up. "Yes? You big bully! You'll beat me now? Shoot me? You will never break me. Never!"

Near the rear of the bus, Dov made his move. Pulled his feet under him, brought his hands around in the same movement, and sprang.

Hussain was only a seat-width away. His back was turned watching Ramz. Dov spun him about and grasped the Kalashnikov. Its muzzle was pointed downward with Hussain's hand off the pistol grip. Dov grabbed that and put the benefit of every set of weightlifters' curls he'd ever done, into lifting the gun upward. When the muzzle was above their waists, Dov angled the gun away from himself, prayed the action wasn't on 'Safe', and pulled the trigger. There was a muffled stutter before the recoil twisted Dov's finger away. Five bullets lacerated Hussain's groin and thigh.

Hussain groaned and sank away. Dov got the gun level and swung the muzzle to find a target. But there was no direction he could fire without killing friends.

Ramz' stream of bullets ripped into Dov's upper body and threw him down motionless. Ramz roared like a mad beast, slung his gun, and lifted Dov's body like a sack of grain. He walked the five or six steps to the back and hurled Dov out into space, to bounce away brokenly.

Then the bus slowed abruptly. Cars ahead were at a standstill.

Ha-Ma'apolim Street and Highway 2

The Netanya police cavalcade cruised smoothly past the red-and-white bus traveling sedately south. Then put on some real speed, intending to beat it to the next crossing, hopefully by some distance

If the bus driver wondered why the police cars had passed him with the drivers steadfastly looking the other way, he didn't mention it to the 30 Turkish tourists on his 'Ali Baba's Magic Carpet Tour,' who were relaxing with the coach's plush curtains drawn against the slanting afternoon sun.

The Netanya men pulled up at Ha-Ma'apolim Street, sent two constables to freeze traffic, then hustled to lay spike-strips. No one had thought about how they'd separate the private vehicle chaff from the terrorists' wheat. Haberman assumed his senior NCO knew what he was doing. Bin-Amr had never been a traffic cop. He hadn't a clue and was just mimicking his boss.

Shabbat was ending. Residents were getting an early re-start. Traffic was backing up on the side streets. Thwarted people who'd been inside all day honked and shouted. An elderly man in a derby-hat slapped his hand on his car's roof, and yelled with a New York accent, "Let's get the show on the road heahhhh!"

The five Netanya officers abruptly realized the mess they had made for themselves. They retreated behind their line of vehicles. Because they'd parked them nose-to-tail, that wasn't much of an improvement. They'd be shooting over each other if a gun-battle broke out.

Lines were also forming on the two. Cars, the terrorists' bus, the tourist coach, and more cars. A loaded down farm truck, more cars, then Lev and his driver. Lev saw at a glance it was a catastrophe in the making.

The trapped terrorists were afloat in a sea of easy targets. Their rifle muzzles were visible at window openings, but curiously they weren't firing, as they had been the length of Highway 2. That surely wouldn't last. If they were to roll grenades under the jammed mass of vehicles, spilling gasoline, and trapping people in flaming steel coffins... It was too awful to contemplate.

The verge between the vehicles and the highway-side fence, if it hadn't been laid with spikes, was wide enough for the terrorist's bus to get around traffic. If their desire to reach the killing zone of Tel Aviv was greater than their urge to cause mayhem here, and he could get those spikes out of the way, they might take the opportunity. But getting there meant passing right by them.

Hellish risky.

But there seemed no choice. "I'm going up there."

His driver blanched. "You're *meshuggah*! (nuts) It's suicide!"

"Just keep everyone else in the cars. Whatever it takes. I'm going now."

Lev slid out of the passenger's door and crouched behind the car in front. Around him he glimpsed confused faces, some children, behind dust-caked window-glass.

If this all goes wrong, I'll never forget these.

The stake-bed farm truck, down to its axles with sacks of alfalfa, was perilously close to danger. But it would give him shelter and a clear view ahead. He'd worry about the next thing then.

He began a fast shuffle and reached the farm truck easily. But bullets ricocheting off the tarmac where he'd been. He figured they'd seen movement, but hadn't gotten a good look at him.

His next two options were bad, and worse. Take the direct route up the middle of the traffic jam and hope he beat their reflexes? Or zig in and out of vehicles? Either way, he was putting people in danger. But he had to reach the tour bus with the closed curtains. In its lee, he'd be able to open the roadblock.

He ran like the devil was at his tail. Gunfire spat before he'd gone three yards. Something stung his thigh. Then he was passing the terrorists' bus itself, smelling the stink. His head was within feet of their guns. He counted on their having to switch windows to aim at him this close.

The last few yards were in full view of what had been the windshield. Bullets punched nearby metal with an odd crushing sound. He dived into shelter like a base-runner headlong into second.

He rested a moment. Then got up with hands lacerated by the road and grabbed the foot-wide strip of spikes They were heavier than he expected. He noticed uniformed bodies behind police cars, and in his Australian twang, shouted, "Are you stupid here you fucks? Gimme a hand for fuck's sake!"

Two young constables uncoiled. They were fully exposed for a moment, but no shots came. The Caltrops were quickly hauled aside. Lev and the two policemen lay down in front of the tourist coach, with Lev praying the terrorists would take the bait.

The Scania nosed out of the traffic and sped up along the outside. Lev glimpsed the driver bent over the wheel by the muzzle of a Russian assault weapon. The holder was a woman in green fatigues, with a short, tangled hair-style. The terrorists veered into the southbound lane and accelerated south.

A tall brutish figure framed in the rear window space, let loose a last spiteful flurry of rounds. Lev had stood up and turned to look back toward his car. A 7.62 x 39mm slug struck the center of the back of his neck. Lev's body dropped to its knees, then pitched forward onto the unforgiving highway.

TWENTY-NINE

Abba Eban intersection, West Herzliya

The tide in numbers, in the geographical zone between Tel Aviv and Herzliya, was turning against the terrorists. Armed soldiers returning to their camps from weekend leave were being picked up at bus-stops and taxi-stands, and transported to the marshaling areas near the expected confrontation point. Off-duty policemen were rushing to their stations to gather equipment, or heading in their vehicles to the rally-points given out in the radio bulletin.

The call for help had reached Tel Aviv too, though not to the public. Two answering the call were Master Sergeant Shem Vilinsky, and his weapons operator, Sergeant Enoch Gavni, from the *Redivim,* the police bomb-disposal unit. They went to the security-forces vehicle-park off Mordechai Namir, signed out their Sunday-Friday vehicle, and rumbled north to assist.

The vehicle was a drab-brown Landrover gun-truck. It had a mesh grill for a windshield, a dozer blade to protect the radiator, and an M60 machine-gun mounted on a post on the flat-bed. It was the ideal vehicle for thwarting terrorist efforts along the Golan and Lebanese borders. The guerrillas' MO was to move M21, 18lb antitank mines from their fields, to where IDF M60 *Magach* tanks patrolled. Shem and Enoch's cure was to stand off a hundred yards and detonate the mine with a stream of rounds.

They were taken under local command at Herzliya and positioned in the middle of Abba Eban Avenue. That was the last very large intersection before Tel Aviv itself, a mile and a half south of where the terrorists had just escaped the roadblock.

Enoch was up on the bed manning the north-facing M60, and Shem was at ground level with his M1 carbine to his shoulder.

Dalal, and the others swaying in the windswept aisle of the Wanderer's bus, saw the truck from over 200-yards away. There was nothing they could do except bully their way past. Khaled was the one who moved his boot onto the gas pedal in case Moshe rebelled. Others aboard thought of the paper-thin metal surrounding them and hunched lower. Phrases from prayers were muttered in both Hebrew and Arabic.

As he watched the enormous, flag-trailing bus charging toward him, Enoch, a normally good shot with the gun when the target was still, realized this was a whole other form of duty. He looked left and right, calculating the room the bus needed to get by. The thought of it going through him didn't bear contemplation. He was the son of orthodox parents, whose daily *Shema* prayer played in his mind. *Hear, O Israel, The Lord is our God; The Lord is one...*

He traversed to make sure the weapon was free-swiveling and had an awful awakening. They'd parked the truck facing their expected target, as usual, so the cab sheltered the gunner's legs from shrapnel. But Enoch's orders were to wait until the juggernaut was in close, then shoot out its tires and engine without hitting the passenger compartment. The height of the cab meant he'd fast lose the ability to depress the M60. He panicked and opened fire when the target was still more than 100 yards away.

Baba'a had faced machine-gun nests as a PLO *Al-Asifa* commander in the early days in Beirut. He'd told his fighters then, "Get in under the machine guns where they can't aim at you." He hollered the same advice over the road-roar, adding, "He won't shoot at the kuffars! Sister make him do it!"

Enoch's first barrage tore up the roadway, wide and yards short. The ricochets screeched away over the roofs of apartment buildings. He cursed and grabbed the pistol grip tighter. The bus was much closer and speeding up. The next rounds ripped at the juggernaut's undercarriage but missed the tires. His third try raked the cabin. Then his nerve broke, and he dropped on the truck-bed to await the collision.

The copper-jacketed .30 rounds perforated the bus's 1/16th inch metal shell like it wasn't there. Some deflected off seat-stanchions and body-framing. Tariq grasped his throat and made a guttural sound. He released one red hand and stared at it in disbelief. Then flopped in the aisle.

A deformed and cartwheeling slug struck Joe Hallwany with an audible thump. He sagged in his bonds. Other bullets slashed at the packed hostages, sometimes passing through to find second and third targets. One went through the frame behind Jeri Karam's right elbow and spent itself in his upper arm.

Then the bus heeled as a yacht does in a storm. Moshe steered it around the bomb squad truck. It settled back on its wheels and continued.

Eastern fringe of Herzliya, 2 miles from Highway 2

Mordy had avoided Highway 2. Instead, he'd looped around to approach the campaign-area from the east. He'd been trying to raise other Yamam officers on their reserved channel, but there was only static. As he rounded Herzliya airport, Zeke got through and rattled off an update.

The stand was to be at Glilot, roughly a half mile before the end of the two. Zeke and one other Yamam man were in route to Aluf Meir Amit Boulevard, on the back side of the ridge that paralleled Highway 2 at Glilot. Mordy knew it from briefings at the nearby Intelligence Information Center. There was parking and only a short climb to the top.

"We've roped in a few soldiers too," Zeke added.

"Make sure they have ammo." said Mordy. "What's the plan from there?"

"They're putting up a road barricade at a gas station just north of the Herzliya Country Club."

"I'll see you there in five."

"Rallying point is a construction shed on the top of the hill."

"Got it."

Mordy made it to the foot of the hill within that time. Zeke's Jeep 4X4 was already parked on the up-slope. He saw his lanky 2IC beckon him on with a big sweep of an arm, before disappearing over the scrubby crest.

The Wanderers' bus had developed a new and harsh engine note from its riddled exhaust, as it lumbered on from the machine-gun-ambush. Inside was a cacophony of cries and groans, and the metallic scent of blood. Much of was that coming from Hussain, who'd bled out from his groin wounds despite Dalal trying to help.

Moshe glanced back once and saw the sharp-faced *mamser* who'd spoken over the tour-guide system was down as well.

Tarick or something.

Moshe smiled, hearing his last gurgles

Then the bus passed an obscuring line of trees on the left. The highway kinked left and straightened. Moshe saw something there would be no avoiding. He put all his weight on the brake pedal, anyway.

THIRTY

Glilot

Mordy reached the ridge top sweating, his legs aching. In front of him between the ridge and the tanks of the off-shore oil terminal lining the coast, stretched the many-times-fought-over-back-through-antiquity, last part of the Sharon Plain before housing-intensive north Tel Aviv.

Highway 2 ran left and right. Wider here, still two lanes, but flanked by horizontal crash-barrier strips on wooden posts. The relatively open ground beyond, once swamp, was patched with thigh-high vegetation, and still soggy in parts judging by a wide and deep drainage ditch. In the near-middle was a knoll where land-clearing debris had been bulldozed into a heap. Medium-height tree-lines crisscrossed the area into fields. A farm road separated the highway from a paralleling row of trees.

In short, a nightmare.

Given a choice between confronting the terrorists here or in the streets of Tel Aviv, Mordy would take it, but he'd trained and fought on similar ground. Loose among this terrain, the terrorists' capabilities would exponentially multiply. Every hollow and tree-trunk could conceal an armed man. He shuddered at the thought of flushing out terrorists among those, and from many other bolt-holes, with night approaching. Still, it was what it was.

Directly below was graded earth marked out into a construction site with white survey pegs. He remembered it was to be a shopping complex with the largest cinema in the Middle East. At the highway-edge was a Sunoco gas station, then a used car lot with maybe a dozen vehicles in front of a sales-shed.

The Sunoco forecourt bustled with policemen and soldiers. They appeared to be taking orders from an army officer in the green fatigues and gray beret of a combat engineer. Men were scavenging for whatever would reinforce a roadblock of police cars parked nose-to-tail.

Seventy-five yards up the highway, past the car yard where the highway kinked and another tree-line masked the roadblock, shiny road-spikes strips spanned both lanes.

The obvious intention was to back up the road-spikes with gunfire from the barricade. There weren't too many ways to slice this *matzah* loaf. He'd have done the same if tasked with making the best of this.

Someone was hollering. By the construction shed he saw Zeke, and one of his Yamam Sergeants named Charlie Moschel. A veteran of London's Golders Green street-fights, an expert soldier, and hard as granite. And four men from the army, holding M16s. They were a mixed batch, judging by their beret colors. Two wore the red of the Paratroopers. *Reassuring.*

There came the thudding of machine-gunfire from the north, answered by Kalashnikov fire, a sound he would recognize anywhere. It galvanized the men below, who sprinted to their posts. Mordy ran as fast as he could toward the construction shed.

Moshe clung to the wheel as leverage for the brake pedal as the Scania crabbed toward the road spikes. He wasn't frightened. Just felt a sense of inevitability. He'd die or he wouldn't. The woman terrorist was screaming. He kept his foot hard down. *What can she do? Kill me?*

Then he remembered the lives of all the innocents in his hands. If he lost control, the bus would roll. He fought to turn into the skid.

Gravity sent Dalal and Khaled staggering. They grabbed the windshield-frame to stop themselves going out through the hole. Tariq's blood-crimson body followed in their wake, leaving a ghastly trail until it too thumped against the front metalwork. Voices shouted and screamed in all pitches. The road spikes disappeared beneath the front, and the bus became an un-steerable missile.

A billow of smoke, laced with brilliant flashes, burst from the gas station forecourt on their left quarter, and from behind the roadblock of vehicles. Beneath him was a harsh grinding of steel tire-rims gnawing at tarmac. The right-front hit the crash-barrier and scraped noisily along it. The Scania skewed out at the rear, then stopped in a haze of smoke and a stink of hot oil and spilled coolant.

Moshe thrust forward the door-operating lever. The front doors opened instantly, and he ran down the steps expecting a flood of escapees behind him. He hurdled the hip-high road barrier and veered out into the field. Legs pumping.

The ground was uneven under the long grass. He stumbled but made it seven or eight more yards before gunfire clattered and bullets slapped at the seed-heads. He dared to hope. There was a massive thump in the middle of his lower back. He pinwheeled, felt his skull strike something hard, then nothing more.

But he'd been alone. The front doors were cable-operated, but the rears were hydraulic. Machine-gun fire had torn away the fluid lines. The door hadn't opened, trapping everyone else inside.

Thirty seconds of quiet passed before a voice spoke up from near the front. Harel Abadi, dust-covered and bleeding, said in Arabic, "Please. Let me talk to them. Let me tell them what you want."

Baba'a and Dalal made eye-contact but said nothing.

"Please! You want something, right? Tell me what and I will ask them. There is no need to fight. Let me tell them!"

Dalal glanced to where Ramz and Hiza'a were nodding. Apart from distant calling back and forth, things were calm at the blockade. *Why not?*

She said, "No shooting. We will try to bargain!" and wriggled her fingers at Baba'a.

He found the folded paper Jihad had given him on the beach. The list of demands. He balled it up and threw it to her.

Dalal said something to Khaled, and he leveled his AKM on Harel. She eased along the aisle on her rear end, reached in and untied his hands. Harel rubbed his wrists while looking at Dalal for instructions.

She scanned the piece of paper. "Tell them we will come out if they put down their guns too. We will release hostages only with guarantees of safe passage, along with comrades we will name. This is a list."

Harel waved it away. "No first they need to know you will not shoot if they don't. I will tell them that, and we will make an agreement, then you can tell them more."

Dalal leaned back, body language telling him he could go.

Harel kept his upper body below the level of the windows, and called out in Hebrew, "Coming out. Do not shoot. Coming out!"

He rose to his full height with his hands raised. Walked to the front doorway. Took a step down, then a step to the ground. He was in sweet, clean, open air.

THIRTY-ONE

Glilot

Mordy threw himself flat on the ridge-top beside his comrades. Watched the spikes and volley of fire halt the bus. Saw one man get off and run west into the fields before falling in a blizzard of rounds. Now another man had stood up inside. He was edging his way into the open with his hands held up.

Mordy had a terrible feeling, and his gut rarely let him down. Those at the barricade would be on hair triggers. He went to shout, "Don't shoot!" but there was a sputter of gunfire. The lone man clasped his midsection and crumpled.

There was a thunderstorm-response from the bus. Glass showered out from windows on the wings of copper-jacketed bullets. Those at the barricade and gas station returned fire full force. The chance of preventing carnage had collapsed with the fallen man.

Then five figures with packs and rifles spilled from the far side of the bus and fanned out into cover, fulfilling Mordy's worst fears. They were Jalal, Khaled, Rami and Wael looking for boltholes, and Fayadh deserting. The little coward threw his equipment, ran until he reached the debris-pile, and cringed down behind it.

Wael aimed for the parallel tree-line fifty yards back from the highway, but his near-drowning had slowed him. Fire from two policemen with carbines marched across the distance and up his body, dropping him lifeless on the grassy road.

The other three found cover behind trees, and in hollows in the ground with line-of-sight to the blockade. They propped their weapons against trunks or on their packs and continued shooting.

The men on the ridge-top were picking their shots. They didn't expect to hit any of the well-hidden terrorists, just prevent them escaping.

Both sides had tracer rounds mixed into some magazines. The early twilight was striped with red from the Israelis, traded with green from the terrorists. The gunfire lasted eight more minutes, despite regular shouting of *"Hafsakatesh! Hafsakatesh!"* (Cease fire) from Yadiel 'Yadi' Popik, the Engineering Lieutenant Colonel in charge.

The hostages were at the end of their endurance. Brutalized by monsters for an hour and ten minutes, and having endured two crashes and the murders of friends, they huddled numbly amid roaring gunfire. But underneath, they were frantic to get off the bus .

Ari Beckman was more worried about his family. Rivka seated behind him with Raviv and Alon had freed his hands. She'd said she and the children were okay, but he didn't believe her, and he was right. The boys were fine, but a near-spent machine-gun bullet had lodged in Rivka's lower back. Moving her legs was agonizing.

Ari whispered, "We have to go. We can't stay here!"

"No. They will come and rescue us, I'm sure."

It wasn't only Rivka's wound holding her back. She'd seen the eyes of the terrorist she'd defied. He'd single her out if she moved. *Our only hope is a rescue like at Entebbe.*

She saw Baba'a say a few words to Ramz and Hiza'a while watching her. She sobbed and hugged the two boys tighter. "They will kill us."

"Maybe they're going to surrender," Ari whispered back.

"They never do that," Rebecca hissed. "They will kill us. I know it!"

Dalal, Hiza'a, Baba'a, and Ramz were ready to fulfill the hostage-death pact made at Es Saksakiye. It would bring rescuers running as wide-open targets, and might even distract the enemy long enough for one or two to slip away. They gathered backpacks. Checked the loads in their AKMs. Baba'a and Dalal moved to the front and waited on their knees in the gore. Baba'a nodded at Ramz.

Ramz swung without hesitation and raked the people in the right rear with bullets. Sapira Lindner and Ori Swartz's bodies jolted and jumped with the impact. He switched left and murdered Eliza and Oskar, in each other's arms. The storm of fire also killed 10-year-old David Abadi and Lina Gerstman, the six-year-old who Dalal had given the candy bar, where they were hidden under the seats.

The brute jammed in a new magazine, then stripped two grenades off his vest. He intended to pull the pins and follow the last three terrorists outside during the five seconds before they exploded. Hiza'a would carry on the slaughter while he did that. But Hiza'a had frozen.

Ramz pulled the first pin. Then Ari came up out of his seat and shoulder-charged him, driving him backwards over the left-side seats. The live grenade dropped and lay spinning beside Rivka's feet.

Ari thought only of obliterating the man threatening his family. But Ramz outweighed him by 40lbs. The Arab battled to get back upright while the

215

Israeli fought to take away the AKM. If he could only get it free, he was an expert with it from his paratrooper-days.

Two rows of seats forward, Ron Marks jumped up from Moira's side and rushed Hiza'a. They collided chest to chest. Ron clawed at the terrorist's clothing but couldn't catch hold. But Hiza'a wasn't holding his AKM tightly. It came easily into Ron's hands. But Hiza'a was too close to use it on him. Ron smashed him in the face. Again. And again. Each thudding blow drove the feckless terrorist further into the seats. Ron reversed the rifle and fired it into Hiza'a's chest.

Ari had Ramz' AKM in his hands at last. He shoved the big man away, then shot him in the face. Then Ari felt his back slam against the ceiling. He dropped back into the aisle, ears ringing. Life had gone into slow motion. It seemed to take seconds to turn his head and look at Rivka and the children. There was only a pockmarked plastic wall and a red-splashed jumble of lacerated upholstery and twisted tubular steel. He looked up the aisle and saw his workmate Ron Marks lying bleeding and dazed.

Ari's lower body seemed detached. He looked down to see his legs resembled boneless, crimson, octopus tentacles. The world sped up to normal. He screamed.

The Two, north of Tel Aviv

Men from every cadre of the IDF, branches of the police, and from all over southern Israel, had been gathering over the last 40 minutes, at two rallying sites. At Kfar Shmaryahu, where the machine–gun truck had been, and where Highway 2 ended. They'd been hearing the regular crackling of small arms fire and were eager to get into the fight any way they could, but had been ordered to wait until there was 'escalation.'

After a series of changes as higher-ranked officers arrived, command had settled on Haifa's Commander Karel Kohler in the north, and Alisha Neufeld in the south. Alisha's men were well briefed. Kohler hadn't yet gotten around to that.

The plan was to form a cordon, and advance inward in columns led by experienced 'point-men.' To capture or kill any terrorist that might have escaped the blockade. And support any hostages that might have gotten away, and free those that hadn't.

Among those massing was a section of Golani soldiers under a uniformed major and a sergeant in civvies. Also Master Sergeant Raphael Levy, leader of the police shooting team, armed with a Remington 700 sniper rifle. And not least, Sergeant Nathan Spiegel from the *Shayetet 13*, the Israeli version of the U.S. Navy Seals.

The police had their .38 Smith and Wessons, a few of the newer-issue Browning 9mm Hi-Powers, and their WWII-vintage, semi-auto .30 M1 and fully-auto M2, carbines. The army officers had 9mm Uzis. NCOs and soldiers carried Colt .223, M16 Armalites. A few soldiers, and the elite-forces men such as Mordy, Zeke and Charlie, up on the ridge, had Galil assault rifles the same caliber.

At 5:46 p.m. there came heavy fire and the muffled thud of a grenade going off in an enclosed space. Terse instructions to "Move in! Go!" crackled over the radios. The groups gathered arms and trotted toward the battle sounds.

THIRTY-TWO

Glilot

The grenade Ramz had dropped bulged 88-191's roof upward several inches above the middle seats on the highway-facing side. The seats and bodies had absorbed the sideways force, but downward it splintered a hole the size of two fists in the Formica-over-plywood flooring. White-hot shards tore open the fuel tank. Gallons of diesel fuel spilled and caught fire. Flames licked up into the passenger cabin. Most still aboard were packed in the rear, but there were ten people alive forward of the explosion point.

Ari somehow dragged his maimed body the few feet to the front doorway and fell out onto the road. He pulled himself a little further away so as not to get trampled. Then tore off his shirt and tied the sleeves around the tops of his thighs before passing out.

First to her feet was Moira Marks, bruised from the jolt of the explosion against her seat row, and deaf from the sound. She dragged Ron down the steps. With his arm over her shoulder, they struggled together across the highway and collapsed on the gas station forecourt.

Marion Abadi got up, frantic to reach her husband outside. With Missy in the crook of her arm, she yanked up her middle daughter Tamar. Her oldest, Rachel, followed. All assumed David would be right behind them, not knowing Ramz had murdered him. At the foot of the steps Marion implored the girls to, "Run! Run!" When they bolted away across the highway, she veered around to the front of the bus and dropped to her knees on seeing Harel sprawled there.

Out behind those six came businessman Mathew Benenson, followed by Arza and Gilad, the young lovers. They headed for the gas station. Policemen got up behind the barrier and encouraged them on, but had to duck again in the face of heavy fire. Mathew was struck and died in the roadway. Gilad staggered from a leg-wound, but stumbled on into safety with Arza.

Marion had found Harel alive but in deep shock. Through her anguish, she knew she could do nothing and had Missy to look after. She ran after the others. Within a few steps she felt a blow as if something had struck her arm, but no pain. Only when she lay behind shelter, did she see a bullet had taken Missy's life. She writhed in grief while a young solder put his hand on her back in comfort.

Half a dozen policemen saw flames rise inside the bus and ran to help. They beat on the door-less side, shouting, "Get out! Get out!" Two exposed themselves to grasp Ari by the shoulders, trying not to look at his lower body. Others picked up Harel by his arms and legs. They carried the horrifically wounded men toward shelter. Bullets tugged at their clothing, and ricochet-chips stung their faces. All made it untouched.

The fire was voraciously consuming plywood and plastic, forcing those remaining away from the heat and toxic smoke. They had to either run through the flames to reach the front door, or force the rear doors open. If they did nothing, it meant an unspeakable death.

Jacob and Lavan Horvath, and after Nina's murder, their surviving daughter Tiva, were among the least injured families. They'd also been comforting Ilan. Jacob picked Ilan up in his large hands, spoke soothingly, and lowered the boy from a window-hole. The lad picked himself up and run toward the car yard. The watching terrorists cared only about killing, even an obvious child. Bullets flew from two or three firing points in the fields. Amazingly, he made it untouched and threw himself down behind the row of cars.

This must have drawn terrorist attention to the Horvaths, but there was no going back. Jacob vaulted out through the same ragged hole and pulled Lavan and Tiva down after him. Then he saw little Junior Forman. Not realizing his family was still aboard, Jacob lifted him down kicking. But Junior was desperate to get back to his parents. He ran away, around to the exposed side of the bus. The three Horvaths ran away across the highway toward the car yard, trailing smoke from singed hair. But no shots came after them. Another struggle inside had dragged attention away.

Those at the barricade were retreating from the choking smoke. Mordy and the men on the crest were the only ones with a full view. They kept up a steady fire, but it was frustrating work. When they pinpointed one target, fire blasted from another location. While they concentrated on the second threat, the first terrorist wriggled like a snake to another tree or hollow.

Flames were climbing up the outside now, and the heat inside was unbearable. Samaritan Johann threw his weight against the rear folding doors. Little hero, Jeri joined him, although nursing his right arm. Then Uzi despite the injury to his good leg. The doors folded aside. Johann and Jeri fell through the opening onto the ground, which in the insane arbitrariness of war, saved their lives. Bullets flew above them and Uzi, in the doorway, fell backward in the aisle.

Out into this hell-on-earth stumbled the next rush of hostages. People faltered and fell, with fewer getting up and trying to get away. Chaima Wolfowitz clung to Rani. Miriam Ehrman was at their heels hugging her backpack Jalal mowed them down from a tree line. The two girls died instantly while Chaima lay writhing.

Judith Hahn struggled to drag out Gabriel. His clothes smoldered, and he was so weak he could barely keep his feet under him. The pair fell into the road, which saved their lives, as gunfire aimed at them ricocheted off the crash-barrier.

There was a momentary pause in the racket while the terrorists were reloading. Rina Coen appeared, towing Nathan, but missing young Benny. Judith had gotten Gabriel back on his feet. Along with Johann, and Jeri with his left hand clamped against his right elbow. The eight climbed the guardrail and stumbled southwest toward the knoll. Rina stared wildly around for Moshe, who lay paralyzed and invisible in high grass. She went right by.

Lastly the confused, the grief-stricken, mothers with traumatized children, and those who'd stayed with incapacitated loved ones, all poured out the rear door with only seconds to spare. Sara, Elon and Aria Perlman had had many glass slashes. Sara had earlier tried to follow Uzi, but Aria wouldn't move.

She'd wanted to throw herself down on her beloved husband, but had to save their children. Else Shwin and Simcha Cohen from bus 901 had tried to get Marta Mizrachi up, but she was unconscious and too heavy. They ducked low to get air and followed the Perlmans. Leah Geffen had a lower side wound but still had the strength to drag little Ephraim, only five. Nathan and Ruth Forman, clutching terrified eight-year-old Jonah, screamed for Junior, not knowing he was already outside. The Gerstmans, who'd been in a trance since watching their daughter Lina slaughtered under the seats, were last off upright.

At last Mordy's groups' suppression fire, and that from men at ground-level who'd found firing points out of the smoke, was having an effect. Brush barely shivered in the fields before bullets responded. In that lull, this whole throng drew air into burning lungs. Then struggled away over the uneven ground and through the cloying vegetation toward the knoll.

But Rami had reloaded and was watching.

Junior arose from some thick grass, saw his parents and ran shrieking towards them. Rami, fearful of death from above, didn't aim. Just jerked up his weapon and held the trigger down. The bullets missed the main group, but knocked Junior down just ten yards from his parents.

There was nothing they or any other escapee could do, but fight onward, then fall down where they could.

THIRTY-THREE

Glilot

When the bloodshed and gunfire ceased, leaving only the flickering flames of the almost burn out bus, Mordy could barely believe that only 17 minutes had passed since the bus first hurtled into sight. But there was more to do. Only he and his companions had seen the battle panoramically, and knew the terrorists' last positions. Acting on that was urgent. Full darkness wasn't far away.

One terrorist lay dead in plain sight. He reckoned there were still six on the loose. *We hurt two or three for sure.*

The enemy lay in hiding within a 75-yard semi-circle west of the bus. But they couldn't keep sniping at movement from this distance with the innocents scattered throughout. That left only one option.

Mordy's Galil magazine contained nine rounds out of the maximum 35. Zeke and Charlie were in similar shape. Fortunately, the soldiers' M16s were the same caliber. A share-around gave everyone a full load. A soldier also went for more.

When he looked up from that, men were approaching in single file from all directions. Then more entered the fields from his left. His heart jumped. They were still half a mile out, but advancing into unseen danger.

Zeke and Charlie wriggled closer. Zeke said, "Can't let them walk into it, boss."

"Nope. Have to signal them to back off, somehow."

"Wish we had smoke markers."

The IDF had their own semaphore for these kinds of situations. Mordy pictured that. *Waving, outlined above the skyline, when at least one of those Arabs is an outstanding shot? No thank you.*

"Few other options, Sir," Charlie pointed out.

"Nope, I'll have to go down there."

Zeke nodded gravely. It was the right call, though that didn't reduce the danger. But that was Mordy. He didn't think about risk. Just his duty. Leading from the front. The reason Zeke would follow the man anywhere. "You and me both?"

"No, I need you here." Mordy knew Zeke would cover him no matter what. Charlie's unflappable presence was also reassuring.

"You Charlie and the soldiers cover. If I flush any out, shoot the shit out of them!"

Mordy had underestimated. The terrain had protected the killers from ground level, but not from above. In fact, most were wounded, though still lethally dangerous. Jalal had lost a lot of blood, where he lay prone in one of the tree lines. Khaled was wounded to the backs of both legs, and could only crawl. Rami had a painful hip wound, and Dalal one to her left arm. Fayadh was untouched behind the debris-mound, begging Allah for the chance to surrender.

Baba'a also hadn't a scratch. He'd kept moving after diving to the ground and found good fighting positions. He was camouflaged with grass and sticks where a bend in the drainage ditch, which was as wide and deep as WW1 trench in places, concealed him from either direction. He had a full AKM and two spares laid out on the bank. Dalal lay behind him, bandaging her through-and-through arm wound using one hand and her teeth.

There'd been no conversation between them. Only an electric tension of knowing the end was close.

Mordy planned a zig-zag run down the exposed face of the hill, and across the construction site. He took a last look around the area. Several people were near the burning side of the bus, jackets over their head. Then others appeared from the exposed side, dragging shapes. Further out, rescuers had reached some escapees who'd run to the southwest. Seven distressed people had outstretched arms. Armed figures from the north had also spread along the far shore below the row of oil-tanks. *Good tactics. If others were as smart, we could wait these terrorists out.*

But with police and soldiers mixed together and no idea what the command structure was, that was too much to expect.

He nodded at Zeke and Charlie, held his Galil hard to his chest and started down the face. He reached the smoke-wall drifting east up the hill, held his breath while running through, then trotted to the rear of the gas station. Yadi Popik, beet-root-red, ash-streaked and coughing, motioned him over. "Thanks for the backup."

Mordy was shocked by the surrounding carnage and could only nod.

There was a row of bodies with their faces covered. Men and women crying disconsolately. Slack-faced children like photos from concentration camps. Medics, with soot-black faces and hair melted into clumps, a pile of medical gear and some running hoses, worked urgently on those just recovered. One slapped at a spark glowing in his tunic. There were two young women. A young boy. A middle-aged woman blinking rapidly and making soft sounds. And something else. It seemed impossible it could be human, yet what must be a chest rose and fell. Martha Mizrachi had been the last one taken off the bus.

Yadi said with depthless sorrow, "The rest still aboard are gone. Eighteen. Nineteen maybe."

Fury welled up in Mordy. "What do you plan to do?"

"Plan? Do?" Yadi wearily waved a hand. "Help these. Wait for reinforcements. Pray to God there are others out there we can still help."

"I'm going out."

"You're crazy!"

"It's got to be done."

"Let's make up a patrol," Yadi said, looking around to see who was available.

Mordy shook his head. "If we go in force, we'll just continue this shooting war. I know pretty much where they are. Perhaps they'll surrender. If nothing else I can signal their locations to those coming." He indicated figures in the distance.

Yadi moved his head from side to side.

Surrender? To one man?

"At least take a couple men to watch your back."

Or pull your dead ass out of there.

Two soldiers volunteered. The three started across the highway, but when only halfway across there came the muffled but unmistakable 'crump!' of a grenade. Somewhere near the knoll. Mordy's pace quickened.

Rami had been changing locations on his belly. His hip was agonizing, but the bleeding had clotted. He'd heard some whispered talk and weeping. *A chance to kill more Jews.*

He heard them again, only yards away, dragged his backpack up his side, and felt for a grenade.

Aria Perlman was the one crying. The shock of watching her loved father killed was wearing off. Sara whispered again from nearby, "People love us. They depend on us. Be strong."

Ephraim Geffen, who'd watched his father break down and be murdered on the bus, lay close by as well. He was shivering and his teeth chattered. Leah was on the other side, trying to comfort him. Aria was sure things were the same in other groups surrounding her, but she dared not move her head to see.

An object hit Aria's shoulder and dropped. Metal and oval and leaking smoke. She gathered her legs and dived away. The ground kicked beneath her. She looked back to see Ephraim, still and sightless. Sara groaned from fresh wounds. Fate had spared her again.

Why only me?

Aria put her face into the dirt and sobbed.

Mordy and his companions knelt by the outside crash barrier where they had a strategic view of the fields. He blinked furiously trying, to improve his poor-light-vision. More support was arriving. One group approached along the highway edge. Other friendlies advanced along the highway from the north. Men were in the trees above the car yard.

Then he noticed a serious problem. A column of men advancing along on the west side of the drainage ditch at a fast clip, heading straight into the heart of danger. They were too far away to hear him shout. He stood and tried waving them back. They stopped, seeming confused. Then started forward again.

Mordy cursed. A single shot cracked out.

Sergeant Nathan Spiegel, the Shayetet 13 naval commando, had grown increasingly nervous. His group were policemen with no combat instincts. The Lieutenant of the Tel Aviv City Police, in charge, was far too eager to get into action. Nathan also felt naked without the Kevlar gear he'd left at his house in his hurry to report.

There was someone over at the road waving urgently. He looked questioningly at the Lieutenant. A bend in the ditch a few yards ahead would be ideal for an ambush, if you were an armed terrorist with your back to the wall.

We should spread out. Wait for the other groups to close the net. We're not flushing game-birds here.

But the Lieutenant motioned him onward. Rank was rank, and Nathan had volunteered to take the point. He took another step. A bright flash ended his existence. Nathan's body pitched down the bank and into the mud.

THIRTY-FOUR

Glilot

Mordy blamed himself. He'd been helpless to prevent the soldier or policeman's murder, but still felt a failure for not moving sooner to head off those in danger. The image of wild tangled hair flying as the shooter dived away into the scrub east of the ditch, was seared for always, into his mind, Shots snarled down from the ridge and flung mud-clods, but uselessly. He solemnly watched the distant body being brought out of the ditch and placed down with a coat over it.

We think we make a difference, but we're all just grains of sand, really.

Black-billed gulls cawed overhead as they flew inland to roost. Mordy looked up, feeling the moment. *I won't forget this. Any of this.*

Now that he had the bereaved patrol's full attention, he motioned them back and to spread out sideways to form a backstop to his right. He spaced out his own wingmen as well, checked the chamber of the Galil one more time out of habit, and moved forward with the gun to his shoulder.

Zeke couldn't stay back any longer. He had to get down there. He ran in the direction of the construction site with Charlie in his wake.

The smoke had thinned, though an acrid haze cloaked the area. The men above the car-yard were straining eyes for targets. Sniper Raphael Levy saw two figures running.

Our people would move cautiously. It must be them.

He led a few inches. His rifle fired itself just as they taught in sniper school. The bullet entered the armhole of Zeke's vest and came out his back. He tumbled. Charlie ran to Zeke's aid.

Mordy was skin-tinglingly aware of his silhouette against the dying fire. *Damn you, concentrate. Look for movement.*

The knoll was beyond of a row of trees, from which a terrorist had laid down deadly fire during the gun battle. He edged toward, scanning left and right. Then jumped inside his skin at shouts of excitement from his right. Men at the end of the backstop-line had converged on someone on the ground. Though they couldn't know the Arab's name, it was Khaled, so weak and disoriented he couldn't lift his weapon. They kicked it out of his hands and dragged him away.

Mordy refocused. Saw a movement among vegetation at a tree-bole. Trained his gun and shouted, "Stand up and come out!"

The movement became an arm swinging a Kalashnikov toward him, then a man solidified behind it. Mordy fired a three-shot burst into the center-mass and ran forward. A large Arab lay face down in salt-stained and blood-spattered fatigues. He rolled the body over with his foot. Lifeless. Picked up the AKM and heaved it a few yards away just the same.

Fayadh watched the big Israeli policeman kill Jalal. He'd also seen the men approach along the ditch before losing their leader. He was being hounded from two directions. But close by were quavering voices and occasional sobs. His survival depended on mixing in with those hostages when the time came. He shrank even lower into his hollow. Begged Allah for his mercy.

Mordy stepped between two trees into full view of the twenty-yard-diameter hump of rubbish. Saw movement and swung the rifle. Made out a woman's face, then children. People began getting up. He'd later memorize the names. Sara Perlman clasping young Aria. Saul and Sharona Gerstman hugging numbly. Others.

"Are there terrorists here? Quickly. Have you seen them?"

Aria pointed a shaking hand. Fayadh got up out of the grass, pleading in Arabic, hands held out suppliantly. Mordy felt disgust.

Rami arose demon-like from bushes ten yards further away. Baby-face twisted into a snarl. AKM to his shoulder. He savored the moment. This big bull-necked policeman was the only threat. The rest would be easy. He'd no doubt he'd die within minutes. This was his last act for his fabled homeland. *Triumphant martyrdom*.

But the policeman was reacting faster than seemed possible. His rifle was almost level. Rami frantically pulled the trigger. Both weapons fired together.

Bullets smashed Rami backward, dead before his back struck the ground. But his Kalashnikov rounds were also on target. Several spent themselves in Mordy's Kevlar vest. One struck high and just left.

Mordy reeled away and dropped to his knees, shoulder turning cherry-red. The two policemen with him rushed to help.

Baba'a took his chance. Hauled Dalal up by her tunic from the marshy tangle and ran toward the highway. She fell behind. Baba'a seized her arm and dragged her with him.

He had no illusions. At most, they were buying a few additional moments. Their destiny was decided the instant Hussain opened fire on the red and white bus. Their dream of a Yáfa martyrdom that the Zionists would never forget was gone. The last possibility was to take as many with them as possible. Dalal had lost her weapon, and he'd left his spare magazines behind. Yet if they could grab fresh weapons, they could still go down fighting.

There was movement to the left. Nine-year-old Benny Coen ran from hiding, screaming for his mother. Baba'a's overwhelmed mind registered only that there was a threat. He waved his AKM one handed in that direction and loosed off half his ammunition. A round struck the boy in mid-stride and sent him down in a small heap.

They reached the crash-ribbon. Scrambled across it. Dalal was gasping. Just a burden now. Shapes of bent-over people loomed at the far edge of the highway. Baba'a's hopes lifted. With the element of surprise, they might yet grab fresh weapons and cause havoc.

The terrorists were racing toward a field hospital where the injured were being brought after triage at the gas station. In charge was a young master sergeant named Ziv Meisner from the *Heil HaRfu'a*, the IDF Medical Corps. Meisner heard boots on the roadway. Looked up from giving morphine to a man with tourniquets around both thighs and, he would have said; unsurvivable leg injuries. Yet the man was here. A man and woman in muddy military kit were charging at him out of the gloom.

Baba'a blazed straight ahead until his AKM clicked empty, obliterating Meisner. He flung the useless thing aside. Ten yards further on, two soldiers were working on a woman on a stretcher. Their M16s lay beside them. *If I can just close my hands around one of those.*

Rifles stuttered. Bullets whipped by. Baba'a felt powerful, twin blows against his upper back. Dalal wind-milled beside him, dead on her feet.

During his last moment, he heard the heat-pops from the fire and the sirens of the Magen David Adom ambulances racing up the darkening Coastal Road.

There was a light brighter than the sun.
All light vanished.

THIRTY-FIVE

Jerusalem, 9th September 1980

The afternoon glowed in the warm sun reflected from golden-stone buildings. Vehicles with guest passes on their dashboards exited Highway 60 in the Mount Scopus district, into the *HaMemshala* (governmental complex) on Clermont-Ganneau Street. Guards guided the drivers to reserved parking behind the security gate of the six-story Israeli National Police Headquarters.

The arrivals signed a commemorative guest book, women received posies, and excited small girls had rosettes pinned to their frocks. An attractive, smiling constable of the Public Relations Service; chaperoned the group along 50 yards of covered-walkway to the panel-lit, tan-tile and beige reception area. Attendants served drinks and finger-food.

Some waiting visitors browsed the wall-displays. A row of recruitment posters gave a visual history of the police back to British times, when a fez was standard issue. One area had the portraits and bios of the six police General Commissioners of the modern era. Nehemia Klein, among them, was present as a guest. Others mingling observed an unusual number of high-level police brass in full parade-dress uniforms, along with an army brigadier and his shoulder-corded adjutant.

An alcove off to the side had 'Remembrance and Heroism' in English and Hebrew in raised metal letters on a raw brick backdrop. A speaker's stand with the blue Star of David, flanked by the flags of the Israeli State and National Police, stood before semicircles of chairs.

The last guest of honor arrived a little before 2.00 p.m. A handsome man with longish hair and a muscular upper body, in a wheelchair pushed by his parents, with a blanket covering his lower half.

People then took seats, and after a minute a tall man with the crossed leaves and stars of Israel's 7th Police Commissioner on his lapels, came out of a side room. Herzl Shafir also wore a small white Yarmulke, as did most men attending. His former rank of an IDF Major General showed in his bearing as he moved to the stand.

"Shalom, Shalom and thank you. Today's ceremony is unusual because the infamous events of March 11th, 1978 were themselves unusual. Not because they were a surprise. Our nation has had to defend itself against dark forces from the moment of its birth. Or for their ferocity. It was unusual for the sheer range of citizens and residents affected. Israelis of every age and from all walks of life had their lives shattered that evil day. And the result would have been immeasurably worse, except for the heroism of a few. Including the ultimate sacrifice of some whose families are here today. Therefore, we have taken the unusual step of honoring armed forces members, policeman, and civilians, all together in this single ceremony."

A woman police sergeant came into view holding a tray covered in eggshell-blue satin. Brigadier Moshe Spelman rose and spoke on behalf of all the services, about Sergeants' Nathan Spiegel and Ziv Meisner. Then with his adjutant passing him the green-trimmed medals in their display boxes, presented the IDF Brigade Citation to their families.

The first two civilians honored also received their medals posthumously.

Shafir pinned Harel Abadi's Medal of Appreciation on his heart-broken widow Marion, who was holding her surviving children Tamar and Rachel. "Harel volunteered to be a mediator between the terrorists and the security forces. He selflessly exposed himself to fire and died of his injuries on the way to hospital. His daughter Gina and his son David also lost their lives in the tragedy."

Dov Dreier's wife Rita, there with their young son and daughter, came forward to receive his Medal of Appreciation. "With complete disregard for his own safety, and with true love in his heart for his friends and colleagues, Dov broke loose of his bonds south of Netanya and stormed the terrorist next to him, seizing his weapon and killing the terrorist in a struggle. During this action, another terrorist took Dov's life."

Almost all the remaining awards were to policemen.

The stylized menorah with twin olive branches, and blue ribbon with red stripes of the Police Medal of Courage, went to the widow and parents of Inspector Levi Boker, with the citation: "Lev led an action at Havatzelet HaSharon that gained enough time for others to create a roadblock further south. Then when civilians became endangered, he exposed himself at great personal risk to separate the terrorists from those in peril, before falling to a fusillade from the escaping bus."

Medically retired Inspector Shimon Ezekiel, now running a security supplies company in Tel Aviv, accepted the Medal of Distinguished Service, for: "Providing support to his commander and working to minimize loss of life before himself being critically injured."

Mordechai Zaks, now a Chief Superintendent, returned a wry grin from the commissioner as he walked forward. Shafir further broke protocol by asking, "Mordy my dear friend, what possessed you?"

He and Shafir *were* close friends. "I couldn't just stand by, sir."

"And you actually drove yourself to hospital with a bullet in your shoulder, in that little rocket-ship of yours?"

"I didn't want to distract from the mopping up, sir."

Shafir shook his head. "You remind me of what was said to the founder of our country's special forces, Colonel Orde Wingate, by his British commander. 'I don't know whether to embrace you for your courage, worry about you stealing my job, or court-martial you for your recklessness.' I'll just say we're the better for having you, and with the thanks of the nation, I award you our highest police honor for bravery, the Medal of Valor."

Then, out of order, the final civilian hero was pushed forward. Shafir broke protocol again, abandoned his podium wet-cheeked, and laid his hand on Ariel Beckman's shoulder.

"I could read out the official statement Ari, but knowing you, it wouldn't do justice to what's in my heart. The pain of losing Rivka and your young sons Raviv and Alon, is barely comprehensible. I can only liken it to having handfuls of your soul wrenched out.

And that's without even mentioning the terrible physical injuries you suffered.

This nation has survived so far, only because of the willingness of citizens like you, to stand up when called and give everything. So we as a people may have, everything.

No one alive has given more. With the gratitude of a nation that loves you, Ari, please accept this Medal of Courage. And may Yahweh keep, and watch over you, forever."

Tunisia, 15th April 1988

The Shabbat-eve sky in which the Deputy Chief of the Israeli Defense Forces had been circling like a demigod for forty minutes, had been so clear, that from the windows of his Boeing 707 AWACS plane he could see the Turkish Bosphorus to the north. Then only needed to turn his head, to watch heat-lightning dance the crests of Libya's Nafusa Mountains.

Fitting, he thought, since his name, Ehud 'Barak,' in Hebrew meant 'Bearer of Lightning'. He intended to strike a blow for his country worthy of his name.

Ehud had a personal reason. During the mopping up after the 1978 atrocity on the Coastal Road, while the dead terrorists were being searched, doubt arose whether Dalal Mughrabi was really a woman. Her tunic was unbuttoned. A snapshot taken of the moment, showed a man who looked like him. Arab propagandists slandered Ehud in posters across the Levant as having mutilated her body. He'd been at Stanford University in California studying for his master's degree at the time. The slur had hurt him. He was looking forward to payback.

But now it was deeply dark, and the cabin was lit by the blue glow of consoles manned by the brightest young men and women of the IAF's 120th Tactical Reconnaissance Squadron.

Ah, to be twenty years younger, thought Ehud, as he watched them work.

They were monitoring a stealth gunboat ferrying 24 members of the Shayetet 13 and Sayeret Matkal, to the waterfront of the city of Tunis.

One of the IDFs fiercest warriors was running the mission. Nahum Lev, a semi-orthodox Jew, was tall, blond, and serious; but a fearless daredevil.

Near midnight, six S13 frogmen went ashore. They secured the area and linked up with Mossad agents who'd entered Tunisia days before on the passports of kidnapped Lebanese fishermen. The Two-Six-Nine troopers, an attack team of eight including Nahum, and two back-up teams, followed in three rubber boats. They boarded Mossad-supplied vehicles and drove to within 300 yards of a villa in the suburb of Sidi Boussaid. They knew its layout intimately, having replicated it in Israel and spent many hours rehearsing a silent assault.

Starting at 1:45 a.m. Shabbat morning, the AWACS plane jammed all communications near Sidi Boussaid, except the commandos' own. Then, resembling a scene from the movie 'Munich,' Nahum, arm-in-arm with a trooper wearing a dress, heels, and blond wig, stepped out into the street. They rollicked up to the sole guard waving a map and a box of chocolates, asking directions to a fictitious party. When the guard looked down at the map, Nahum shot him in the head with a silenced pistol from the chocolate-box.

The troopers went about their assigned tasks like well-oiled machines. Some locked down the area while the main team forced entry into the villa's basement. Another guard' and a gardener unlucky enough to be spending the night, were also killed before the shooters worked their way up through the villa's three floors.

They cornered Khalil al-Wazir, Abu Jihad, at the top of the stairs, along with Intissar, who had Iman and Hanan beside her. He'd been tipped off and was armed with a pistol, but had stayed too long watching video coverage of the Intifada he was orchestrating in Judea and Samaria. The commandos filled his chest, then his head, with bullets, but spared his family, which was more than the evil little man ever did for anyone else. They took fingerprints and photographs, then left the way they came, burned their vehicles on the beach and sailed home to Israel without suffering as much as a stubbed-toe.

Ehud heard the code words proclaiming complete success' from aboard the soaring AWACS plane. The aircraft broke orbit and banked gracefully toward the Israeli coast. He smiled blissfully, doffed his headphones, settled back into his plush leather seat and closed his eyes. He imagined himself at the keyboard of his cherished Yamaha grand piano, playing Brahms. Sonata Number One maybe. Bittersweet. He gestured with his hand as if conducting.

AUTHOR'S NOTE

This novel is based on a true story, the tragedy Israel calls 'The Bloody Bus', and is commonly known as the Coastal Road Massacre. I extend my deepest respect to those who were involved that day, and those who lost loved ones. I am deeply grateful to Natan Taig in Jerusalem for facilitating so many important contacts and for spending hours with me on Skype and in person. Also, many thanks to Avriham Peretz at the Egged Bus Museum in Holon for sharing his knowledge unstintingly, and Yossi Hochman and his daughter Orya for their living example of the triumphant power of life. The 12th Israeli Commissioner of Police, Assaf Hefetz, will always be my personal hero